WILD JUSTICE

WILD JUSTICE

ROBERT MCCAIG

CUTTING EDGE

ISBN-13: 978-1-952138-47-8

Published by
Cutting Edge Books
PO Box 8212
Calabasas, CA 91372
www.cuttingedgebooks.com

ONE

AFTER TWO YEARS of roving with John Starr it still pleasured me to size up a new town. I liked to loaf around one, stop at the store and saloon and blacksmith shop, listening to the talk. I liked to sit on the hotel veranda, watching the long-distance spitters and listening to their damn' lies. I liked to study each new face, trying to guess the story back of the blank windows of the eyes. Always too, and always, I made my judgment of the way a man tied down his holster, or I looked for the slight sag a belly gun made. And the way a man held his hands, and toed in his gait. Little things that might keep me alive.

This game of mine wasn't one John Starr cared for. Maybe just the difference between twenty and thirty-nine. But John Starr didn't seem to give a plugged nickel whether he was in Laredo or Belle Fourche, just so he got cash on the barrel-head and a chance to throw down on renegade and outlaw. But me, I liked to savor every place I met up with.

This Miles City now: it was cowtown. It looked cow and it smelled cow. It was raw and noisy. I liked the busy, bustling way of it. I sauntered down the main street, thinking that the coming of the railroad the year before hadn't dried up any of the rich juice of the town. The bull teams were still furrowing the hard-pan of the roads. I met wolfers and trappers in from the high country. As they passed, the stink of them was fit to knock a man down. The swaddies from Fort Keogh roamed the sidewalks, looking for drink or trouble and finding both, though it was long to payday.

I could feel the difference between this place and the wild boom towns I had known with John Starr, the towns where the very breath of a rumor would blow every man out of town and into the high hills between sunup and sundown, and leave the raw camp a grinning skull among the aspens. Death wouldn't come to Miles like that, I decided. Not as long as folks hungered for beef.

Just ahead of me a door flew open. Two men tumbled out of it into the grit of the street, beating on each other like Paddy beat the drum. They rolled and squirmed and wrestled, with none but me paying attention, until neither man could raise a weary arm to strike again. They lay in the dirt, gasping like fish out of water, the sweat runneling the grime on their faces.

A man in a dirty white apron came from the saloon. He was carrying a horse bucket. Without ceremony he emptied it of water on their heads, and went back inside. Bedraggled now with mud as well as dust, the men struggled to their feet. One grabbed the other's shirt front and drew back a knotted fist. Then he shook his head wearily. He lowered the threatening hand and, instead, put his arm around the other's shoulders. Leaning on each other, the two stumbled over the sidewalk, lurched through the batwing doors. Laughing now, the two of them, like hyenas.

The sheer foolishness of the two besotted rascals tickled me so, I wasn't watching where I was going. I turned a corner and bumped solidly into someone. I caromed off the blind wall of a building, catching my balance. I turned to see the man I had run into. He was maybe two years older than me, slim built, with a beaky nose and the glint of a killer mustang in his eye. He stood braced, his thumbs hooked in his gunbelt, giving me the stony look.

He had a soft unpleasant voice. "You take up too much room, fella."

"Sorry, mister, my fault," I told him, which was only right.

Maybe I should have bowed low, or at least looked him in the eye. But I was too busy staring at the pretty yellow-haired girl beside him. She was about the handsomest thing I'd seen in a coon's age, maybe longer. She must have known him and I were walking the knife edge of trouble, for she looked scairt. But she still made a sweet picture. I smiled at her, though she didn't smile back.

"You think that's enough?" the man said. He waved a hand. "Well, it ain't good enough for me. You ain't packin' an iron. Go get one."

I stared at him. For certain sure he was spoiling for a fight, but I didn't aim to let him get my dander up. I grinned. "Not me, mister," I said. "I'm a decent, peaceable citizen. I said I was sorry. I'll say it again. That should do it."

He shook his head, a dark hot shine on his face. He made a tentative movement.

"Please, Shan," the girl said. "The man apologized. Don't seek for trouble."

He shouldered her aside to move toward me. His walk was slow and deliberate. His left hand reached for the front of my coat; the right palmed his gun butt.

If this ranny thought he could pistol whip me, he had another think coming. John Starr had taught me never to use half-measures. I stepped in instead of back. I brought a knee hard into his crotch, chopped the edge of my left hand across his right wrist, and drove my right fist full into his face. He screamed, and spun like a tee-totum. He dropped into the dust, his knees drawn up to his belly. He made odd little choppy grunts of pain.

I reached down for his gun. The girl knelt beside him, lifting his bleeding face from the clogging dust. I flipped the loading gate on the .44 and shucked out the shells, disgusted with a man who would let a decent weapon get so rusty and gummy with dirt. I dropped the empty gun beside him.

The girl looked up at me, her eyes blazing, though there was, I thought, a little fear in them.

"You should be proud of yourself, cowboy," she said hotly.

"Then in your judgment I should stand hitched while an armed man beats me to death?" I asked pleasantly.

She recoiled. "I mean—well, you don't fight fair. The way you hit him and all—that's the way wild beasts fight. You've half-killed Shan."

"He asked for it, all the way," I said. "When he comes around, miss, tell him to throw that rusty sixshooter away, else he'll get himself killed sudden, likely by some school kid, the way he uses it. Here ..." I reached toward her.

Automatically she held out an open hand. Into it I dropped the brass cartridges from the man's pistol. "So long miss," I said. I doffed my hat politely and turned away. Without looking back I walked around the corner.

For a minute or two I was right pleased with myself. But as I went down Main Street, I began to have doubts. Maybe I could have handled this Shan in some other way. Maybe I could have— I swore at myself. Girls, decent girls, anyhow, were sure a puzzle to me. I guess because there wasn't much room for such in the life of a roving lawman.

I walked into the nearest saloon. The bartender set a mug of beer in front of me and silently took my money. The heavy mug was wet and slick under my hand as I sipped the frosty bitterness of the brew. I found myself still brooding over the ruckus in the street. I hoped it didn't come to John Starr's ears. We tried to be as quiet and inconspicuous as possible when we were starting out on a new job. Well, I couldn't undo it now. I drained the stein and called for another.

I watched the bartender draw it, for I always took pleasure in watching an artist at his trade. I admired the quick sure flirt of the wrist to start the flow, the studied inattention until the very moment the mug was full, then the swift, careless motion at the final second to close the tap. He sent the mug sliding down the bar to me, the creamy collar of foam just kissing the rim, not a drop of the cold brew wasted.

Drinking it slowly, I stood with a foot on the brass rail, my body turned half toward the front door. There was an off chance that Shan might come seeking me with blood in his eye, though my guess was that he backed into a hole somewhere, licking his wounds. Still, John Starr had taught me that carelessness could kill a man.

Down the bar I caught the drift of an argument between a young puncher and an older man I had noticed as I came in. They were at that stage of drink where wisdom flowed from their lips with ease, the sound of it echoing pleasantly in their own ears.

"You name Abilene—sure Abilene is tough," the older man was saying. "Never insisted she wa'n't. So is your Dodge City tough, so is your Rapid, so is your Ogallala. But they been tamed, ain't they? And who tamed 'em? No goddam' army, I say. Jest one good man tamed 'em, that's who. There ain't no town too big or too tough for one man, if he's a damned good one."

"But that's the point, Cork. That malpais out there, it ain't no town. One man starts skyhootin' around in them washes and flats and coulees, he gonna get his goddam' head shot off'n him. Them owlhoots, they're here today an' gone tomorry. They won't truckle to no law. You ask me, they're tougher'n hell. They got that whole country right where they want it. You couldn't get me to ranch up there, no sirree. Nor even work on one of 'em. Why, looka, Lazy L's got work for a bronc stomper for all summer. Needs one the worst way. Me? I need work. But not at Lazy L, Cork. It's right on the edge of outlaw country."

"But I say one daggone good salty he man—"

"Cork, it's gonna take a army to clean out them rustlers, an' I don't mean the swaddies from Keogh an' Maginnis, neither."

"You've got the right of it, kid. Them fourflushers down in Wash'n'ton don't give a hoot in hell for what happens to us folks out here. They won't never turn the troops loose."

"That's a gut, Cork. I tell you, the rustlers is top dogs along the Missouri. The Live Stock Association played it smart when they voted to leave 'em be. They…"

Cork began to laugh. "Son, I didn't know you was such a babe in the woods. You b'lieve everything you hear? You think Kohrs and Stuart and Grant Stevens and Fergus and men like them will knuckle under just like that? Sure, they voted down the young fire-eaters like Teddy Roosevelt and the Marquis de Mores. But in that back room at the Mac-queen House, well… Son, I ain't big enough potaters to get into the inner circles of the association, the sanctum sanctorium as you might say. But, son, I got ears. And I got eyes. And if I don't read the signs of a big cleanup, dam' sudden to boot, you can call me a halfbreed. Somebody says John Starr—"

The mustached bartender put down the glass he was polishing and moved with deliberate speed down the bar. Leaning close, he said something to the older man in a low voice. Then he moved away.

For seconds there was a taut, embarrassed silence. Then Cork said: "Yes sir, son, as I was sayin', you think twict before you buy that hammerheaded grullo off'n Matt. The jughaid's got plenty of bottom, I'll grant you, but that long jaw on him…"

I put down my empty mug and walked out. On the street, in the crisp spring air, I found myself grinning at the small scene. It proved the Live Stock Association carried plenty of weight in this man's town. Which was a nice thing to know, since they were the ones who had hired me and John Starr. Different from Pyramid, I thought, where the whole town hated the law and sneered at the men who enforced it.

I turned past the Mercantile, walked by the Macqueen House, and on out toward the livery barns. Miles City was dull quiet. Down south they would call it "siesta"; here in Miles it was "between trains." Always quiet between trains, they would say, between trail drives, between paydays. True now, I decided. Miles was snoozing. The splintery wooden sidewalks were empty. A few cow ponies drooped at the hitch rails, patient save for stamp of hoof or shudder of hide to discourage flies. The sun was warm, but the southwest breeze had a small nip to the edge of it. Across the wind drifted the faint mellow notes of a bugle from Fort Keogh.

There was nobody at the barn, not even the hostler. The horses were bunched in the sun in the corral, sleepy and quiet. I found a seat from a dismantled buggy against the barn. I sat down, stretching my long legs, digging my boot-heels into the soft duff of the yard. It would likely be a while before John Starr got through and came back. I pulled down my hatbrim to shade my eyes and tried to doze.

Of course, a pert lovely face, a mane of hair butter yellow in the light, intruded into my thoughts. To me, at my age, girls were about the most interesting, although the most puzzling, creatures on God's green earth. Who was she? Who was the man Shan, and what was he to her? What had she thought of me, Tod Morgan? At times I pictured myself as a younger version of John Starr, saturninely handsome, sure of himself, quick, tough, and deadly. But I had the uncomfortable feeling that the girl had looked past my pretense and seen the Kansas farm boy with manure on his boots. I admitted ruefully that there was only one John Starr. I could never be his equal. Nor was I sure I wanted to be, I admitted secretly to myself—and felt a certain shame at making the mission.

Yet the contempt of the girl was only another indication of the void that lay between us and ordinary people. I had said something of the kind to John Starr when the people of Pyramid had proven so aloof during our enforced stay there. John Starr, his bullet-shattered leg stretched out on a hassock, had merely laughed.

"Forget it, Tod," my uncle had said. "Mankind is divided into sheep and wolves. Though we are on the side of the sheep, guarding against wolves, people see us as inimical. They use us but they don't like us. Our kind makes them feel uncomfortable. We're different, and they can't understand us." He paused, then added, "Nor by this time do I understand the sheep."

I hadn't entirely understood the parable, though I caught the aptness of the comparison. John Starr was as lean and fierce and as single-minded on the hunting trail as any wise old lobo. There was always the moment when guns flamed and men lay suddenly dead on the chill ground. I dreaded it, and I think in a way my uncle dreaded it too; for always thereafter he was for a while like a man drained of will.

It disturbed me. I wondered if there was something lacking in me, so that I couldn't deal out justice impersonally. I was as lean and hard and lupine as John Starr. After two years of constant practice at his never satisfied insistence, I could track as well as he, and was nearly as fast with hand gun and rifle. I hated all I had seen of the cruelty and rottenness of the criminal element, as much, I think, as John Starr did. But for me there was always the hope that even in the worst of men there lay some modicum of good. If so, it might be worth trying to save.

John Starr, on the other hand, had one rule: extermination. He had his reasons, to be sure. Where my hatred of crime and criminals came from the head, John Starr's came from an implacable heart. When each trail ended, there was no satisfaction in it for him. He was left merely with a driving urge to get on to the next one.

I shook my head, tired of thinking. The sun was warm on my face and my closed eyelids. From the barn came the not unpleasant ammoniacal smell of horse. Somehow it carried me back two years to the beginning of my travels with John Starr. I saw again the gray dull day when I had ridden Prince out of the yard at the homestead for the last time, with the walleyed mare dragging at the lead rope. And John Starr waiting below on the trace while I rode up the Kansas hilltop alone, to stop beside the fresh graves of my mother and father.

TWO

JOHN STARR, with the surprising sensitiveness he often showed, had left me to say my farewells alone, though under one of the mounds slept my mother, Starr's only sister. I remembered that now, recalling how lost and forlorn and desperately sad I felt, for only two days had passed since, within hours of each other, both my parents had gasped out their lives with what the Kansas country people called "galloping grippe." I remembered the raw wet earth of the heaped mounds, and how I had shivered in the icy Kansas wind.

I had pulled on Prince's rein, turning him so that I could look back. The gray shanty blending into the pewter sky and the leaden earth suddenly seemed an alien thing, though most of my life had been spent in it. I had not even regretted the sale to the neighbor of the pitiful accumulations of our lives. Save for John Starr I would have walked away and left them.

Prince had been my father's horse, and a good one. He moved restlessly in the cold wind. But before I turned him, I stood up in the stirrups for one last sweeping look from southwest to northeast. I saw again the monotony of the prairie under the ragged sky, its ugly flatness broken only by the tangle of willows where the creek meandered through it. Far to the right rose the wheel of smoke from a neighbor's chimney. Suddenly I had seen all I ever wanted to see of it. I urged Prince into a quick trot down the knoll.

Now I know that John Starr had no desire to have an eighteen-year-old sodbuster kid tagging along after him into the harsh confines of the frontier which circumscribed Starr's world. But his rigid New England conscience dictated that he set my foot on the straight path. To do so, he had to take me with him. Once, much later, he told me that he thought I would otherwise have drifted into the Sand Hills, to work for some jawbone outfit, sooner or later to take the owlhoot trail. He was right, too, for in spite of my decent upbringing I owned a sneaking admiration for the James boys, the Youngers, and Sam Bass and Hardin and the other famous gunfighters. Following John Starr, though, soon changed my mind about the wild bunch.

As I rode the trail behind Starr, I realized the rare good fortune that had brought him through Kansas on one of his infrequent visits to my mother just when I needed him most. I watched this hawk-faced man, with the pliant power in him like a *bois-d'arc* bow, with awe and a certain fear. They said that both bad men and good walked softly when the word was up that John Starr was riding their way.

He reined in his horse now. "Tod, my mind isn't easy about letting you trail along with me. It isn't any life for a kid. Yet I don't know any other course. So you can ride with me on one condition—that you follow my orders to the very letter."

"I'll sure do that, Uncle John," I said eagerly. "You just tell me to jump and I'll jump, you bet."

He looked at me with a thin smile, firming the black line of his mustache with the knuckle of a forefinger.

"The day will come when you'll curse yourself for answering so glibly," he said. "But I'll hold you to it. Tod, because in my business a man's first mistake is usually his last, I'm going to work you day in, day out, until you know the rudiments of how to stay alive. I'll see that you practice until you're ready to drop. That will be your choice. Any time you get your fill and want to make your own trail, you can. It makes no never-mind to me. Savvy?"

"You don't scare me, Uncle John. I'll work and I'll learn. Why, I can ride anything that runs on four feet. And I can shoot, some."

He laughed at me. "Tod, boy, I'll give you the riding. I don't believe I ever saw a better hand with horseflesh. But as for shooting—Tod, the cheapest little hardcase in a backcountry cowtown would kill you before you could spit."

I must have looked dismayed. He leaned over and patted my shoulder. "With work we can change that, though," he said.

I nodded, feeling the hard sure strength in him. From it I drew strength to myself. I knew only vaguely, then, the almost legendary reputation John Starr bore along the frontier. He was the lawman of Hungry Camp; he had brought the law to Kerryville in three wild days. He was the John Starr who had stood rock calm through the flame-lanced seconds of the Antelope Stable fight, wounded but still on his feet at the end, while Cord Leason and three of his renegades lay dead in the dirt of the corral. And there was the tale of John Starr's tracking and execution of Tug and Cale Rondout. But more of that later.

Before we reached Colorado, my arm ached with weariness from the constant drawing and aiming with the heavy .44 Starr had given me. My shoulder was sore from the recoil of the Winchester rifle as we burned box after box of cartridges.

I learned by heart his lecture on how to handle and care for my weapons.

"Human nature is a puzzle, Tod. Here is a man who claims to settle his differences with a gun. Yet the very thing he depends on for his life, he lets get rusty and pitted, fouled with grime. An exception? No, Tod, the majority of men neglect their weapons, strange as it seems. So by taking a little simple care, a man has that much edge to start with."

He taught me the side draw, not caring for the cross draw that was more popular. He showed me how to use a rifle with lethal skill, and how to reload it quickly from any position. We had lessons on the niceties of knife work, its cuts and guards and parries, and he taught me how to throw a weighted blade. He showed me the tricks of rough and tumble, lessons which kept me stiff and bruised most of the time. He taught me the deadly use of the feet for attack and defense, the *savate*. And he made me do these things over and over, as a virtuoso practices on his violin.

"There's no time to stop and think, Tod," he warned more than once. "You and your weapons must be united into a single precision instrument. Only practice can achieve that coordination."

"But, Uncle John, it gets so tiresome!" I cried.

He jerked his head toward our back trail. "You know the alternative, Tod. I have no strings on you."

"All right," I said with a sigh. "Give me the pistol again."

By the time we reached Toadtown I knew more about weapons and their use than the ordinary man ever learns. But I was still no expert. Nor would Starr let me employ my budding skills in that grim affair.

Before Toadtown I had imagined John Starr and myself as sort of range-land paladins, going about righting wrongs, perhaps rescuing lovely ladies from wicked villains. Toadtown, as ugly as its name, brought home the bitter truth. It jolted me to learn that bringing law to the lawless was a rough and brutal affair, full of pain and anger and sudden death.

In Toadtown my uncle killed two men with his own hand. He directed the hanging of another, and ran a dozen lesser offenders out of town, all within thirty-six hours of the time we first rode down the crooked main street. We were through and gone, camped for the night in a cleft of the Rockies high above the town, before my numbed mind could cope with the wild burst of action. Now I sat by the fire, sobered and a little sick at the remembrance of things seen.

"Uncle John, are you always so sudden with a gun?" I asked.

"It's the quick or the dead, boy," he said mildly. "The minute I let sentiment control my trigger finger, I'm through. You must learn, Tod, that these criminals deserve not the least consideration. Mankind is too sickly soft about them. Such men should be exterminated from the face of the earth. You will do well to remember that."

"But they're still human beings, aren't they?" I asked brashly. "There must be different degrees of evil. Surely the man who has sinned once is less guilty than the man who has sinned a lifetime."

With the flowing smoothness that always marked his movements, John Starr was on his feet and standing over me. His face was dark and terrible in the firelight. I cringed.

"They are devils from hell, all of them!" he said. "You get this through your head—outlaw and renegade and murderer can expect no mercy from me or mine. Seven years ago two of them broke my life in little bits and threw it in my face. I vowed then that with what was left of life I would hunt them across the length and breadth of the West. And I will do it as long as there is breath in me."

"But why, Uncle John? Why?" I cried.

Instead of answering, he dropped to the ground on the far side of the fire. He hid his face in his hands. Finally he looked up, the flame catching a glint of moisture in his eyes.

"You are of my family, Tod," he said, calmer now. "Otherwise I would not even tell you, the only kin I have left. After I have told you, never speak to me of it again. And I do not wish this story repeated. Remember that."

His tone was so bleak that I shivered.

"I promise, Uncle John," I said. And I meant it.

He told me then the story of Mary Reade. Sometimes his voice dropped so low I had to strain to hear him; sometimes it rose loud in anger. Twice he broke off to go into the circling darkness, as if to regain his composure. Long before he was through, not only did I understand his motives, but I felt as ready to kill as he was.

John Starr had come to Elmville, he said, after a successful career in freighting and railroad construction. Still a young man, he had bought the general store and set up a livery business as well. His abilities and pleasant manner had brought him success; he had become moderately wealthy and something of a pillar in the community. More, he had won the heart of Mary Reade, a young and pretty teacher at the town school. They were to be married in June. On the spring morning that changed John Starr's life, there seemed to be not a cloud in his firmament.

That was the morning that the Rondout gang hit Elmville. They hit it in the manner which the James boys were to try at Northfield three years later with such disastrous results. Since the James boys had a rough plan and a sort of schedule, and the Rondouts had nothing but brute force, the Northfield disaster did not hold a candle to what happened to the Rondouts. Their own stupid brutality was their undoing, for they stopped at the edge of the town to kill a man for no reason. The firing warned the citizens well in advance of the gang's strike on the business district. When the Rondouts stormed into the center of town, the bank had locked its vault, stores and saloons had stashed their cash and valuables, and everyone was grabbing for guns and ammunition. A Nebraska town like Elmville could count hunters, plainsmen, and ex-soldiers who knew firearms and who in many cases had killed their men before that day.

The Rondouts smashed their way into the bank, then murdered the cashier and teller. They set off a blast of powder that laid one wall of the building out into the street but left the vault unscathed. They swore and cursed and pounded on the tough steel even while the townsmen under the command of John Starr were working up the street, sweeping the Rondout riffraff ahead of them, picking them off wherever they holed up.

The situation finally penetrated the thick heads of Tug and Cale Rondout. They grabbed the wallets of the slain bank employees and scuttled out the rear door to their horses. They quirted their mounts out the west road, not in the least concerned with the predicament of the few remaining members of the gang. They raced through the back streets, with men in pursuit of them as soon as they could obtain horses.

The school stood in a grove at the west edge of town. Well ahead of their pursuers, Tug and Cale Rondout rode into the schoolyard. It was recess time. Seeing those wild men riding in, the children screamed and huddled like frightened sheep. Mary Reade stepped defiantly between the children and the Rondouts.

"Don't you dare lay a hand on one of these children!" she cried.

"All right, we'll take you!" Tug Rondout yelled. He reached from his saddle and hauled her across his horse in front of him. He pulled her to a sitting position, an iron arm around her slim waist. The reins in his left hand, his right holding a Navy Colt, Rondout waited until the posse burst from the trees. He put the muzzle of the pistol against Mary Reade's temple, and sent his horse racing down the Scottsbluff road behind his brother. John Starr, sick at heart, held up a hand and stopped the posse.

Within the hour Starr again took the trail, this time with three of his friends and a Piute tracker named Crazy Walker. They were well armed and deadly of intent. They followed the thin track that led always away from the towns, into the thinly settled lands, and finally out into the desolate area north of the Platte. Crazy Walker said the tracks showed the girl was still with them.

Fearful of missing the trail, John Starr and his men stopped until the first light of dawn. They rode now with a terrible urgency, knowing that the harder the Rondouts were pressed, the more dangerous they became. The outlaws were calling the tune. They had several courses open to them. Late in the day they took one of them. They discarded Mary Reade.

The curtained dust was hanging heavy in the lifeless air of twilight when Crazy Walker found the girl beside the trail. Mary Reade was a moaning bundle of bloody, torn clothes, with only a scrap of life yet in her. Starr's voice dropped to a hoarse whisper now, though he could not or would not tell me the unthinkable things the Rondouts had done to the girl. She was conscious from time to time, and she must have told him her grim story as he sat holding her hand through the long twilight. She died just as the last light fled from the sky.

At dawn, on a grassy hilltop, they buried Mary Reade. Unhampered now by caution or scruple, they raced on. They followed the dim track ever northwest, against a horizon where gray clouds began to bank in rolling masses. By mid-afternoon Starr and his men were pressing on through the downpour, scanning the dimming trail. Finally they had to hole up in the abandoned cabin of a wolfer. The rain lessened by dawn to a heavy drizzle. They started out in the watery gray light. Crazy Walker led them uncertainly for a mile, then another. At last he straightened up. "All gone," he said, with a helpless shrug.

They swung a big circle in the rain, then another. But it was hopeless. Five bitter, angry men turned back to Elmville.

Within a week Starr had sold out his business. He and Crazy Walker holed up at Starr's farm at the edge of town. All day, every day, the sound of gunfire pounded through the hours. Ammunition went out there by the tens of cases. Shipments of arms, with the labels of Eastern gunsmiths, arrived. One by one a herd of the finest saddle horses appeared in John Starr's corral. Then, one day, Starr and the Piute were gone.

At that point Starr stopped speaking, to sit staring into the fire. The silence grew intolerable.

"Then you caught them, Uncle John?" I asked softly.

My voice snapped his mood. The hooded look dropped back over his hawk face. He was retreating into his inner hell of suffering.

"They paid," he said curtly. "Douse the fire, Tod. It's time you rolled into your sougans."

I can complete the story now, for I gathered sufficient information over the years to get an outline. Tug Rondout's body was found hanging from a beam in an abandoned stage station west of Fort Smith. And outside was a mound of earth with a headboard that read, "Crazy Walker—a good Indian." It was known that in late fall Cale Rondout was found on the Cheyenne trail with a neat bullet hole in his head.

Starr never laid down his guns. Wherever the law needed him, he hired them out, until the name John Starr became pure magic.

THREE

I LEFT THE warmth of the Montana sun and the soft whisper of the spring breeze lull me into a doze. How long I slept I do not know, but I showed the two years of hard training my uncle had given me when a light footfall sounded beside me. I was on my feet, spinning away from the bench with an Arkansas toothpick from my neck sheath already in my hand, when John Starr chuckled.

"Not bad, Tod. A right fast knife draw. Best of all, you didn't forget and go for the gun you're not wearing. For a sleepyhead, you'll do." His tone changed. "Saddle up, kid. We're moving out."

"Jake with me," I said. "Did you get—"

He gave a quick hand sign for silence, frowning. I shut up. I should have known better. I saddled Prince and Roller, packed the walleyed mare and Starr's perky little mule. When I was through, my uncle took a stick and sketched a map in the dirt of the corral. He gave me instructions, then scuffed out the lines with a boot sole. He was standing looking after me as I jerked on the mare's lead rope and rode west down the sleepy street.

I crossed the Tongue, then rode north past Fort Keogh to the ferry. The ferryman grumbled a little at taking a lone passenger across the sullen spring spate of the Yellowstone, but an extra silver cartwheel made him take to his sweep with a will. As I rode off the flatboat on the north bank, I noticed the frayed end of a broken strand twisting out of the stout Manila rope. I pointed a finger at it. The ferryman just shrugged, then grinned. He poled the flat away from the bank, out into the rush of the current.

Your neck, mister, I said to myself. I rode on up the steep grade of the wagon road and over the rimrock.

I set up camp on Sunday Creek. Supper was all ready when John Starr rode in. Afterward, I went about my chores while he lit a cigar and moved up closer to the fire. I put the things away, spread the bedrolls, and went down to the creek to check on the horses. They were tethered and quiet. With some reluctance I turned back toward the red eye of our small fire.

It was a beautiful night. The bottomless sky was ridged and furrowed with stars. The western rim of the horizon was still faintly outlined in dayglow. The night breeze sprang up, just strong enough to ripple the curing buffalo grass in faint susurrations. Somewhere far off a coyote barked, the harshness of his wail mellowed by distance. From nearby came the blat of a calf, quick with terror. Then silence.

I stood still, my face turned toward the cold glow of the stars. I had an odd feeling that Starr and I were this night about to cross an invisible line of decision, with no turning back after we had crossed it. I felt a sudden, almost overwhelming urge to throw the saddle on Prince and head back for Miles before the moon came up. But of course I walked back to the fire, and sat crosslegged on my bedroll.

"It's good pay, and in gold, Tod," my uncle said, his face inscrutable in the faint flicker of the dying fire.

"Who needs pay, if we can rid the world of a few badmen, eh, Uncle John?"

He took me literally, missing my attempt at sarcasm.

"You're learning, kid. Some day this frontier will know real law. But until then decent men must administer their own brand of justice." He touched the shining walnut butt of his colt. "Now we're beset by riffraff and renegades, Tod. Killers, thieves, murderers. We must stop them, we can't let them live—"

His voice was rising in the wild way that scared me when I heard it. I stopped it the only way I knew.

"But the job, Uncle John. You haven't said what I have to do."

The outburst was cut off, as if it had never occurred.

"The stockmen and merchants and freighters of this area are tired of being abused and preyed upon, with raids and thefts and killings. They've had a bellyful of it. They aim to stop it. Our job is to help in a grand cleanup of all of central Montana, clear to the Dakota line—and past it."

"Vigilante vengeance, you mean?"

"Better organized than that. With the power and prestige and cold cash of a powerful group solid behind it. It's a big thing, Tod. It's a wonder it hasn't leaked out."

"I s'pose," I said, thinking of the episode in the bar in Miles City.

"Grant Stevens, the spokesman who hired me, insists that everything be done as legally as circumstances permit. He says we must have positive evidence before punishment. He won't stand for the working off of old grudges in the name of justice."

"Well, a man might get shot trying to corral evidence, but it's worth a try. How long have we got?"

"Stevens figures on the first part of July. By then the spring roundup will be well over. He figures that will show up plain evidence of mavericking, brand blotting, and other thievery. Added to the other evidence, it ought to hang a few men."

I did a little figuring. "This is the first week in May. Two months, then. It isn't much time."

"Time enough," Starr said. "These renegades have been bold enough in their operations to leave a broad trail. As long as they held the whole region under their control, they didn't have to be careful."

"Proof's something else again, though," I grumbled. "How did these outlaws grow so bold?"

"Circumstances, mainly. In the early days it took a tough breed of men to buck this country. They were trappers, wolfers, prospectors, buffalo killers. Now the buffalo are wiped out, the railroad has squeezed out the river boats and their wood yards, and most of the Indians are cooped up on reservations. The hard customers don't fit into the world of the cattle and sheep business, or civilized living at all, for that matter. So they're holed up in the bottoms, making a desperate living any way they can. But they and their ways are doomed, Tod, even if they don't realize it yet."

"What evidence are we looking for, mostly?"

"These men aren't choosy. They'll rustle, blot brands, rob caches, hold up stages, rob travelers. The big thing, though, according to Grant Stevens, is the traffic in stolen horses. The cattle rustling is picayune beside this."

"Now you're down to cases. How do we begin?"

"By being strangers to each other, for one thing. You didn't let anything slip in Miles City?"

I grinned at him. "You trying to teach Grammaw how to suck eggs? Course I didn't."

"Good. I've got a cover act picked out; I'll be a remount buyer for the British cavalry. I'd like to see you get a job on one of the ranches."

The conversation in the saloon came back to me. "Why, I know of a place. Spread called Lazy L, right on the edge of the Missouri River breaks. Heard a cowpoke in Miles say they needed a bronc snapper in the worst way."

John Starr pulled a paper from his pocket, leaning toward the dying fire to study it.

"Here we are—Lazy L, B. Lowall, owner; Rance Kiley, foreman. Funny, there's a star against Kiley's name, but not Lowall's."

"And the star means?"

"Suspect by the association. Tod, if you can get on there, do it. A fine vantage point for our purpose. You head over there in the morning. It's beyond Silver Spring a ways."

"How will I keep in touch with you?"

"I'll be circulating around the country as a horse buyer. I'll make Lazy L, look over the ground. If favorable, I'll try to visit it often. So close to the breaks, Lazy L should be an ideal spot for observation."

A little later, when I rolled into bed, I was thinking of our errand. And I remembered the cowboy's statement: "Man's going to start skyhooting around in them washes and flats and coulee's, he's gonna get his goddam' head shot off'n him." I shook my head. They say a man can't live forever, but danged if I wouldn't like to try.

We were up, and had eaten and packed before the flush of true dawn had worked its way below the tips of the scoria mounds that ringed our camp. Our farewells were brief. Leather creaked as Starr swung up into his saddle. The mule snuffed a little as my uncle tightened the lead rope.

"Take care of yourself, Tod," John Starr said. With a wave of the hand he rode north in the pink-gray light. He did not look back. I was pleased but a little scared that he had seen fit to let me go on with my part of the job without his dotting every *i* and crossing every *t*. This was the first time he had really turned me loose, so I had some pardonable pride.

Minutes later I was mounted and riding toward the Musselshell. I sat straight, looking around me with a new assurance. If John Starr considered that I was ready to graduate from his harsh and unrelenting school, I knew I could take care of myself in any company.

I laughed now at my vague fears of the night before. The morning sun struck warm against the back of my heavy coat. I knew I would have to doff it soon, but not quite yet. Far ahead I could see the candle glow of the distant Crazies, with the pink sunrise flaring off their snowcaps. Nearer, the country was fair, newly shot with green. In the bottoms the early willows marked the small creeks with verdant coils. Cattle were moving in the open, steers somewhat gaunted by the winter, the old cows belligerent over their leggy calves. I observed, in the spirit of my dream of my own ranch in the far future, that there were blocky

Shorthorns and Durhams among the cattle. I nodded approval of the good sense of these ranchmen in breeding better strains. The old Texas strain was cheap and hardy, but they were all bones, horns, and hide.

I thought of how much I had changed since I left the Kansas ranch two years before. John Starr had taught me well. I had known hard men and renegades around my Kansas home, but the men of Toadtown had awed and terrified me. By degrees, as my education progressed, I learned how to handle them, and eventually to despise them. Besides the use of weapons, John Starr taught me some of the amenities of life, something of manners and gentle customs. He opened for me the world of books, turning me into an avid reader. I, who had known only the bare boards and bare teachings of a Kansas country school, read of the open world, of far places and strange names and the doings of great heroes and great scoundrels. For this I shall never fail to thank John Starr.

After Toadtown, we moved to the Idaho diggings. Starr cleaned out the boom town of Ophir and broke the Stag Layton band of road agents. We made our way into the Coeur d'Alene, west again, and south to the John Day country. I saw in wonderment for the first time the stark ugliness of the Nevada desert. We dropped down to Beatty and Bullfrog, crossed to Pueblo, then went north again. We took on a job for John Iliff, to find out why one sector of his vast Colorado empire was losing money. The foreman of that ranch died under John Starr's guns. What Iliff did with the man's accomplices we never learned.

In northern Utah we were set on the trail of the Lussy gang, who had a penchant for knocking off gold shipments. We were two days behind them at Helper, a single day at Twin Falls. North we rode, for a day stumbling through a lava field that was plain torture, full of shapes so twisted and grotesque they resembled a landscape on the moon. Hard on the trail, we rode fast, ever north through hot days and chill nights, the sagebrush without end, the mountains high and serene on each side of us. Along the cold sweet waters of the Salmon we caught the Lussys. Uncle John laughed to see me duck at the keening *spang-g-g* of a ricochet.

He killed two of the Lussys and the other two gave up. We brought them with the unopened treasure chest across the alkali flats to Fort Hall. There we loafed and rested and fished for a week, until a wire came for Starr. It was from the Wyoming Stock Grower's Association. We headed east that night.

We came into Cheyenne by dark, nor did we leave until starlight. My uncle, wise in the ways of the malefactor, did not doubt that the moccasin telegraph could tap even the outer circles of the august association. We did not tie up with its agents until we got to Publicker Creek. There we broke up an organized gang of thieves and rustlers. Two of them who fled were trailed by Starr and me all the way to Grand Island before we got them behind bars. On the way back, we met in Ogallala a Texan with a burning mania to kill John Starr. My uncle waited until the man's pistol was clear of the leather before he put a bullet into each of the man's arms.

Our work must have pleased the association, for they assigned us to Pyramid. Two range detectives had already been killed there. Two others had sold out or disappeared in a rat's nest of outlaws, rustlers, and plain common thieves. The renegades had much of the country on their side, for gold or blood or favors granted. Nor was the local law any better.

Gathering evidence was simple, for their contempt was such that they flouted the law openly. John Starr and I turned in a report that named the names and dates and places. At an appointed day we met in the town of Pyramid with three other association detectives and half a dozen United States marshals armed with guns and warrants. We struck swiftly, riding down on ranch after ranch. We brought the ringleaders into Pyramid and held them under heavy guard.

The sheriff tried to break the men loose. When he saw that this wouldn't work, and figured he was on the list, he forted up in the jail with two of his gunslinger deputies and three tough nuts from the rustler crew. We poured lead into the building from all sides, cutting down the sheriff and another man. The door opened and the chief deputy and the other three came out in front of the jail. John Starr and I and two of the deputy marshals went to meet them.

There wasn't any fancy stuff. Everyone began shooting. The whole world seemed a hell of flame and gun smoke. When it was over, the four of them were down in the dust. Of us, the marshal next to me was clutching a wounded arm, and John Starr was on one knee in the dust, his face gray with pain, his hands clamped around his left thigh. A doctor came, and under his supervision we carried John Starr to the hotel. The doctor shooed us out.

I went back to the jail. The two badly wounded men were gone. The chief deputy and the outlaw who had been my target were lying dead. I shoved my way through the knot of morbidly curious people and looked down at the bodies, especially at that of the younger man, knowing my bullet had killed him. He was not much older than I. I turned away and stumbled toward the hotel. I had let the life out of a man who, regardless of his past, was a human being. I gained little consolation from the fact that he had been trying to do the same to me.

We stayed in Pyramid because of Starr's broken thigh. By winter the town and the region were raw and chill and ugly. The people were as bitter as the weather. They held it against us for separating them from easy crooked money. Even the doctor, who was well paid for his visits, seemed to take pleasure in hurting Starr when he examined the wound. Finally I became disgusted with his manner and the aroma of bourbon that emanated from him, paid him off, and told him to get out. From that day on, my uncle got better.

When we left in the spring, I didn't know the names of more than a handful of the Pyramid townspeople. Nor did I have any wish to know. We traveled leisurely along the high clean valleys of the Tetons, under the massive peaks. We were well equipped; we did not force our pace; and John Starr's ailing leg improved daily. For exercise, we hunted and fished. We saw the snowfields shrink and the wildflowers begin to star the meadows. We moved north into the region once called "Colter's Hell," now a national park named Yellowstone. We marveled at the great steam spouts of the geysers, the boiling springs, the weird rock formations, the unearthly blue of the lakes. We gasped at the unforgettable sight of the Yellowstone River plunging over its immense fall into the deep canyon.

We found that though the politicians had created the park on paper, they had balked at money. The trails were much as the elk and deer had made them, which suited me and John Starr, though we found it best to be careful where we pitched our tent, lest boiling water come up under us during the night. But I vow that until trails are cut and bridges built, few Americans will ever get to see the marvels of this wild, strange country.

We moved on past the Firehole, reached Mammoth Hot Springs, and so left the park. Some day, God willing, I'll visit that land of wonders again.

In the little railroad town of Livingston, Starr sent a telegram. The next morning his answer came.

"Pack up, Tod," my uncle said. "We're heading for Miles City."

FOUR

H EADING for Lazy L, I wasn't much worried about the cover
job. I've always had a hand with horses. Even last winter,
in Pyramid, while the local people had hated my guts they had
grudgingly hired me to break some of their horses. And still
more grudgingly they had admitted I did a good job of it.

I rode into Silver Spring in the early afternoon. It wasn't
much, a long store building of peeled logs chinked with white
clay, a small cabin built similarly, a well built stable, and smaller
sheds and outhouses of scrap timber or sod. I dismounted in
front of the store and looped Prince's reins around the hitch
rail. The pack mare grunted and blinked a walleye at the place. I
pushed back my Stetson and walked up the steps.

The old-timer who sat there with his chair tilted back on its
two rear legs glanced at me speculatively. He looked away, pinned
a grasshopper to the porch floor fifteen feet away with a stream of
ambeer, and gave me a wordless grunt.

"This is Silver Spring, isn't it?" I asked.

He nodded, his cold blue eyes unwinking.

I mopped my face with my silk neckerchief. "You wouldn't
have anything cold to drink around here, old-timer?"

He dropped the front legs of the chair to the floor with a
thump. Reluctantly he got to his feet, moving toward the door.

"Wet, anyhow," he said, holding the screen open. "This is
'bout the first day that would warm a man's bones. Kinda caught
me with my pants half-mast. When she gets honest-to-God
hot, I keep a bottle or three of Milwaukee lager, the pure quill,

down to the ice-house. But now you'll have to settle for air-tight tomatoes."

"Sounds good, mister," I said, following him in. "This your spread?"

"Dam' betcha," he said, pride in his voice. "Quite a layout for a busted-down puncher, eh? They said I'd never make 'er. But it turned out Bart Stoker was a natural-borned storekeeper. Dam' shame I wasted forty years of my life lookin' at the back end of a million longhorns."

"That's the dirty end, all right, Mr. Stoker," I said.

"I'll tell a man." He reached for a can of tomatoes and set it on the counter in front of me. "That'll be two bits, cash," he said pointedly. "Y' ain't stony, are you?"

For answer I tossed him the coin. I picked up the hatchet that lay on the counter and drove two crisscross slashes into the top of the can, then forced down the sharp points. Lifting the can I took a long gulp. The flat, slightly salty liquid just hit the spot. Holding the can, I slung a hip on the counter, taking my ease, looking around. The store had the usual miscellany of the frontier trading post, and was well stocked. But I saw no bar. My eyebrows must have raised.

The old man reached under the counter and got an opened box of soda crackers. He motioned to me to help myself. "Stranger, ain't ye?" he asked.

I nodded.

"Think it funny I ain't got no bar, do you? Saw ye looking. Well, sir, I consider a bar's more trouble than she's worth. So I just tell 'em: 'You want supplies, groceries, canned goods, harness straps, Stetson hats, gunboots or tin thin gamajigs, you get 'em from Bart Stoker. You want to lap up firewater, raise hell, shoot holes in merchandise or men, carry on like a Blackfoot renegade, go to Burnt Rock. Over there, Ingersoll likes things his way. Me, I like 'em my way. Any time you don't like my way, I got a loaded Greener under this yere counter!' Stranger, a man couldn't be fairer than that, now could he?"

"You don't mince words, Pops, that's a gut," I said, grinning. I fished the tomato pulp out of the bottom of the can with my knife point. "Guess you have to. They tell me this country's hairy and hard to curry."

"More so than I cotton to," he said. He fixed me with his hard blue eyes. "You like that? Or don't you need a quiet spot on a back trail, where the U.S. marshals never go?"

"Dam' if I do," I said, setting the empty can on the counter. "I'm not on the owlhoot trail, Mr. Stoker. I'm a pore but honest bronc stomper looking for a spot to light. I'm hoping to run across somebody in this neck of the woods with some real tough cayuses they want busted to a fare-ye-well."

"Now ain't that something?" Bart Stoker said, relaxing. "I wa'n't trying to offend ye, stranger, but there's too dam' many of the wild bunch around this neighborhood now. Bronc stomper, eh? Happens I do know somebody might have work in your line. On Lazy L, twenty-five mile or so northwest of here."

"Draw me a map, would you? I'd appreciate it. My rates are reasonable, my work guaranteed. What kind of a ranny is he? The owner, I mean."

Stoker chuckled. "Well, *he* ain't no kind of ranny, mister, because *he's* a *she*. The widow Lowall runs Lazy L. Does a hell of a lot better job of it than her late husband, Tall Tom Lowall, did when he was alive."

I was taken aback. "A woman owner? Well, I'm not so sure ..."

"Don't say no jest yet, kid," Bart Stoker pleaded. "You wait here for a bit, because I'm expecting Miz Lowall to ride in here most any time. Some stuff she ordered come in on the Lewistown stage. So wait and talk to her, anyhow. It won't do a mite of harm."

"All right, I'll wait then. Say, my name's Tod Morgan."

"Pleased to know you," the old man said, giving me a firm, wiry grip.

I leaned against the counter. "What's the story on this Widow Lowall, Bart? She's had trouble?"

"A young whippersnapper like you ain't skeered of trouble, is he? There just might be some, at that. Shan Kiley won't bust the broncs, but he'll make it tough for you on Lazy L. Jest on general principles and consarned meanness."

"Gimme a can of those peaches," I said, wiping my knife blade on my Levis. I opened the can and dug out the golden sections of sweet fruit. "Now, Pops, begin at the beginning. Who's this Kiley?"

"His dad is Rance Kiley, foreman at Lazy L. This Rance was a great pal in his day of Tall Tom Lowall. They was cut out of the same cloth. Shan is worse'n his dad. Rance will work, at least. Funny thing, though. Bent thinks Shan is a little tin god."

"Now, who's Bent?" Lowall, the widdy's only son, spoiled brat. He'll be on the wrong side of the law one day if he don't steer clear of Rance and Shan Kiley, and their cronies over to Burnt Rock."

"Her son, you say? This Mrs. Lowall, is she young and pretty, with hair like a buckskin pony's mane?"

"Beth Lowall? Naw, she's a durn good-looking woman, all right, and not so dam' ancient. But she's got dark hair. You're thinkin' of Sunny Lowall, the daughter. Swell little gal, too."

"The job's a gone goose then, Bart. Shan Kiley had a mind to pistolwhip me on the street in Miles yesterday, but I gave him his comeuppance. The girl was there—she didn't take to it kindly."

"Now, now, wait up, Tod," Bart Stoker said. "How'd it happen?"

I told him.

"Lord, man, Sunny wasn't sticking up for Shan," he said when I finished. "It's jest—well, she does a lot of reading; she's got her purty little head full of romantic ideas. It jest seemed to her you took advantage of pore li'l Shan."

"Him with a gun and me unarmed?"

"If she figgered you were the underdog, she'd pull jest as hard for you," he said. "She's like that."

"Well, if I get the job, I hope she thinks better of me," I said. "I'm right taken with that young lady."

"Don't blame you. Hope the Kileys don't climb you too hard."

"Why doesn't Mrs. Lowall toss the whole kit and caboodle of 'em off Lazy L? Get rid of them for good?" I asked.

"Needs Rance, I guess. He knows horses, and Lazy L's mainly a horse spread. Besides, he was pals with Tall Tom; claims Tom sold him a fifth interest in the ranch before he got hisself killed up in that saloon brawl in Billings. Beth Lowall finds it easier to let Rance play it his way rather than stir things up. The Kileys got plenty of tough friends." He leaned closer. "You want my guess, she's scared spitless of the Kileys, but figgers they're insurance against the wild bunch."

Outside, a dog barked, warning without anger. The old man moved to the window, looked out.

"Told you to stick around, kid; here's Miz Lowall now."

We went out on the porch, the screen door slamming behind us. I wanted to see the woman who could run a horse ranch. I didn't believe it, much.

She was coming down the slant of the trail, sitting side-saddle with easy grace on a chestnut mare. She wore a riding habit of a coarse, serviceable blue material, but she wore it with an air. Beneath a cocked hat with a sweeping plume, her face was golden tan. She halted her horse in front of the store.

Before I knew how it happened, I was off the porch and making a stirrup of my hands to help her down. She stepped into it, with a clear free laugh, the weight of her body thrusting at me for a moment.

"Thank you young man," she said, with a brilliant smile and the shadow of a curtsy. She took my arm as we went up the steps. "Bart, is the new medicine helping your rheumatism? Good. And did my package come?"

"It sure did, Miz Beth," he said. He held the screen open. I followed them inside, finding it hard to believe that this beautiful woman could be old enough to have a daughter the age of the girl I had seen in Miles.

When Bart Stoker gave her the bulky package, she hugged it in her arms with a little cry of joy. Laughing, she turned to me. "Only a woman could understand, young man, the pleasure of receiving the material for two new party dresses," she said. "Especially to dress her pretty daughter. Out here in this wilderness our courage needs bolstering—and a new dress will do it!"

"I cain't keep up with that, Miz Beth," Bart Stoker said, grinning. "Exceptin' you and Sunny alluz look A Number One to me. Say, this young feller's named Tod Morgan. Been waitin' for ye—claims to be a first-class horsebreaker."

Her laughing face went suddenly serious. Her gray eyes widened. "Are you truly looking for such work, Mr. Morgan?"

"I'll bust any and all critters you point out to me," I said. "My work is guaranteed. You won't find any flinchers or shiers, any bridle fighters or spooks, after I'm through with 'em."

Her face was alight. She touched slim fingers to my arm.

"What is your contract price?" she asked.

"Why, the regular, ma'am. Readied for the rough string at five dollars a head. You want any of 'em purely gentle, fit for ladies or tenderfeet, cost you another five on top of that."

"We won't have much of that. There isn't any profit in putting a ten-dollar finish on a thirty-dollar horse. Maybe a few, though. In any case, I have about two hundred head to rough break. What do you say?"

"Suits me down to the ground," I said, holding out my hand to bind the bargain. She gave me a firm, warm handshake.

Bart Stoker was grinning like a Chessy cat when we rode off. Mrs. Lowall waved a hand at him and took the lead, riding easily in the awkward sidesaddle. I tugged at the pack mare's rope, and followed.

We were two miles down the road before I mustered the courage to say: "I figure I'm right lucky to catch on a big job like this first off, me just riding this way from Miles on spec. Seems some local boy would have grabbed it."

"You don't understand this country, Tod," she said, frowning. "We have a considerable floating population. They find work degrading. They make some kind of living by their wits—and their guns. My son Benton is a good rider, and he could do some of the breaking; but he is so fond of the frontier life that he dodges the job. Shan Kiley, the son of my foreman, could do some of it; but I've seen him savage more than one horse, and he won't do it to mine. They are my cash crop. And Art Cobb and one or two more from over Burnt Rock way could do it. Except, as I said, it's too much hard work. So, Tod, your arrival is a minor miracle."

"I'll do you a job, Mrs. Lowall. You won't regret it."

"I'm sure of it. And you'll like Lazy L. Only—if Rance or Shan Kiley troubles you, let me know."

"If they trouble me, Mrs. Lowall, you'll know it. I'm not a trouble hunter, but I don't let anybody hooraw me."

"I believe that," she said, chuckling. "Most of you bronc snappers are pretty salty individuals. But, do you know, I don't think I'll even warn my crew."

"Maybe you won't have to," I said. "This Kiley, now—I tangled with a fellow in Miles yesterday—dark, with a beak of a nose and a shifty eye. Aimed to pistol whip me. I changed his mind for him."

"Shan was in Miles, all right, with my son Benton to pick up Sunny, who was getting in on the train from Minneapolis after a visit to her grandmother. Was—was Bent in trouble?"

"Didn't see him at all. But there was a girl with Kiley, I remember now. Seems to me she had yellow hair and dark eyes."

Her laugh was stippled with delight. "You, Tod Morgan! A boy your age carries away a much clearer picture than that after seeing my daughter Sunny for the first time. Isn't she an angel?"

"As to that, I couldn't say, ma'am. She was right put out at me yesterday."

"Just what did you do to Shan?"

"Oh, I sort of swarmed over him."

"Good for you. But, at the ranch, walk softly, Tod. Take care of trouble, but don't start it. For my sake. Rance Kiley is—well, I can't talk about it, but there's danger in it."

Her face was serious. I thought I caught a hint of terror in her eyes.

"I'll keep my lip buttoned but my powder dry," I told her. "Don't worry, ma'am. I aim to keep busy snapping broncs. Likely I won't have time for much else."

"If—if things only don't pile up," she said, frowning. She touched spur to the chestnut. "Come, Sunny and the boys should have been back from Miles long since. I'm anxious to see her."

Lazy L, as we looked down on it from the south ridge, was a pleasant, well kept ranch, though it obviously wasn't the headquarters of any cattle king. There was a long low house of adzed logs, chinked with clay. A large bunkhouse, a barn, and various sheds and outhouses sat in a grove of large cotton-woods, with everything looking in good order. A creek, wide and swollen now with the spring rains, wound beyond the yard in a swirl of greening willows. A few cows grazed in a fenced pasture, some Rhode Island Reds scratched industriously in the barnyard. A man carrying a milk pail crossed the yard in the long shadows.

"Lazy L," Mrs. Lowall said softly. "How do you like it, Tod?"

"A right pretty spread, ma'am. You own it? The land, I mean."

"We have patent to a full section here along the creek, and another beyond where you see the big cottonwoods. I worked hard for it, Tod, and it's mine. Or was." There was bitterness in her voice. She gathered her reins. "All right, bronc snapper, let's go."

We rode down the hill into the yard in the cool twilight.

FIVE

I HAD stripped the pack mare and was unsaddling Prince when a man came at me out of the inky shadows.

"What the hell you doing?" he asked bluntly.

I turned to face him. He was a man maybe forty, forty-five, lean and knobby, with a heavy mustache and a beak of a nose like that of young Kiley.

"Unloading my gear," I said.

"Then pack up again, damn you!" He stepped closer. "We got no room for saddle tramps around Lazy L."

"You just go tell the boss lady that, then. She hired me."

"The hell you tell! I ramrod this spread. Get that duffle back on them nags and get your tail out of here! Damned sudden."

That was enough for me. I moved toward him.

"You must be Kiley. So keep your shirt on, man. Mrs. Lowall hired me to snap broncs at so much a head. You got any gravel in your craw, don't work it off on me."

"So, a smart cookie. Listen, cowboy, you've got just three minutes to be out that gate and gone."

"And after three minutes, if I'm still here?"

His jaw dropped in genuine astonishment. "What's the matter with you, man? I'm Rance Kiley."

"I've heard of Wyatt Earp and Jesse James and John Starr," I said, shaking my head, "but dam' if I ever heard of Rance Kiley. You chaw up a man for breakfast every morning, do you?"

Sharp etched in the slanting light, his face twisted with anger. His hand swept toward his gun.

"You want to get your head blown off?" I asked pleasantly, the muzzle of my pistol pointed at his head.

With exaggerated care he moved his hands wide of his body, the fingers spread. He looked at me a long minute, studying me as if to fix my features permanently in his bad book. Finally he said: "All right, gunslick. There's the bunkhouse. Find yourself a spot. It's no skin off me if Mrs. Lowall brings in a hardcase to fight broncs. But get this one thing, sonny; you ever pull iron on me again, you better be ready to use it!"

I stepped into him. I brought the muzzle of the .44 up under his chin, with enough pressure to move his head back. I'll say this for him, he didn't flinch. After a minute I stepped back, let the hammer down, and shoved the gun back into the leather.

"I'll go one better, Kiley," I said. "You make one motion, ever again, to draw on me, an' I'll kill you."

Our eyes locked. At last he turned on his heel and walked rapidly toward the main house. I finished caring for my horses, hung my gear in the harness room, and lugged my war sack into the bunkhouse.

Most ranch bunkhouses were boars' nests, dirty and stinking and crawling with bugs. This one looked clean and smelled clean. A man might know Mrs. Lowall wouldn't tolerate dirt or vermin. I saw her touch in the crisp scrim curtains on the windows, in the well scrubbed planking of the floor.

Two of the bunks were made up, the upright apple boxes nailed to the wall beside them filled with men's personal effects. I took over an unoccupied bunk, made it up, and stowed away my possibles. After that, I sat down on the bunk, feeling uncertain, and damned hungry, for my stomach was touching my backbone.

Mrs. Lowall hadn't said anything about supper. In my pride, I wasn't going up to that house without an invitation. Besides, it might make trouble for her if I didn't let that raunchy straw boss of hers cool down before I met up with him again. So I tightened my belt, lit the student lamp on the table (an improvement over the usual smoky lantern) and dug a book out of my packs. It was one John Starr had picked up in Miles, *The California and Oregon Trail,* by a fellow named Parkman. Things had changed since he wrote it, mostly for the worse. As far as I had gone, I had a tremendous admiration for the frail little man who bucked that rough country.

A tentative knock came at the screen door. I looked up, blinded for a moment by the shift from light to darkness. Then I shoved my chair back, for in the doorway stood a girl, lovely in gay flowered muslin, her hair in a yellow glow in the lamplight.

She gasped in surprised recognition. "Why, it's you!" Then, in indignation, "What do you think you're doing here?"

"Your mother ought to put up a sign," I said mildly:

" 'Come to See Tod Morgan, the New Bronc Snapper. Lazy L Bunkhouse, 6:00 P.M. to 5:00 A.M., No Admittance Charge.' "

"Well, smarty, how would I know?" she asked. "I s'pose it's all right, then. Mother just said there was a hungry cowboy in the bunkhouse, and to call him to supper."

I put on my vest and took my hat from the peg. I held the screen door open for her.

"You still owly because I wouldn't let your beau gunwhip me in Miles?"

"He's not my beau! And I don't look to see any man pistol whipped. It was only that you—you were so savage!"

I shrugged. "It's a tough dollar, miss. That Shan isn't any shrinking violet, either. Nor his pa, who also does not like the way I wear my Stetson, or something."

She shook her head, started to say something. Then we were at the house. She led the way into the kitchen. Mrs. Lowall was there with another woman.

"Here he is, Mother," the girl said. Then, as if in confusion, she hurried away through an inner door.

Her mother looked after her, half smiling. She turned to me. "Mrs. Ledger, Tod, my good right hand on this ranch. Mamie, this young man must be starved. He will have an awful opinion of Lazy L hospitality."

The gaunt elderly woman nodded without speaking. She dished up hot food for Mrs. Lowall and me, durned good food, too. If Lazy L fed like this all the time, it was a long cut above the usual cow or horse ranch. I saw with approval that Mrs. Lowall ate as heartily as I did. I hate a fussy, picky woman that eats like a bird; give me one that makes no bones about honest hunger.

Over coffee I said, "Your ramrod had some objections to me working your horse herd."

"So he said. But it didn't get far with me. I notice you're still here."

"I don't scare easy, Mrs. Lowall. I see you have two other men here, by the looks of the bunkhouse."

"Two good boys, Ox Pendroy and Red Beckett. They've been out for two days gathering some of the herd down in the bottoms. They should be bringing in some material for you tomorrow."

"The quicker the sooner. Because my poke is flat."

She laughed. "Like all horsebreakers. If they saved their money they'd own the ranch. More coffee, Tod?"

I shook my head. She began gathering up the dishes and

Getting down to business, I could see why Mrs. Lowall could ask good prices for her stock. They were well bred, sleek, bright of eye and smooth of movement. They had already lost most of their winter shagginess. I chose a bright bay for my first demonstration. I dabbed my noose on him on the second throw. Not liking the feel of the Manila, he reared, striking at it. He pawed the dust of the corral.

Ox and Red came in to give me a hand. Soon we had Reddy (I named the horse instantly, as all bronc busters do) up against a taut rope. When it choked him, he quit lunging. So we snubbed the rope around a stout post I had set in the corral for just that purpose. Reddy strained back, bracing his feet. Inevitably he threw himself. I flung myself at him, half-hitched a rope around his jaws for a hackamore. With this purchase I managed to bridle him before he knew what was up.

I released the rope. Reddy lay there, sucking in the good air. While he was still studying, I threw crosshobbles on him, leaving only one rear hoof free. I let him struggle to his feet. When he tried to lunge away, he threw himself in the dust of the corral. Once more he tried it, and fell heavily. Then he had the lesson learned; he stood there quivering, streaked with sweat and dust, waiting for what might come next.

With the reins and rope, I worked him until I had the saddle-blanket on him. It was even more of a chore to get the forty-pound saddle on him, but I made it. I kneed him in the belly and snugged up the cinch. Talking softly to him all the time, I reached up and grabbed his ear. With a solid twist on it, I nodded to Red Beckett to get the hobbles off.

I eased up into the saddle, settled my rump firmly into the leather and my boots into the stirrups. Then I let go of Reddy's ear. I felt him coil under me like a steel spring. He shook his head. He took two steps to make sure the hobbles were gone. They were. He exploded.

He went up in a stiff-legged arc and came down like a pile driver. He tried to get his head between his knees. I yanked up again. He blatted like a mad bobcat and fished for the sun. He spun, reversed, drove hammer hoofs into the duff of the coral. He unloaded his whole bag of tricks, and it was a stacking them in the galvanized iron sink. I hurried to help her.

"Thank you, Tod," she said when we were through. "We need more boys like you on this horse ranch. You'll start work in the morning?"

"If the horses are in," I told her.

I was almost to the bunkhouse before I realized that there was something more than mere joshing in her tone. There was an undercurrent of pleading, almost of desperation. I don't have the second sight, but I had the feeling of dark shadows clustering about the ranch.

When I went to bed I slid my six-shooter into the space between the ticking and the bunk rail, ready to my hand. For I was too young, I thought, to die (even knowing that at eighty a man would still feel that way). For a moment I was panicky, missing the strength of John Starr. I tried to push fear away, telling myself that I was a man, and that I could handle rough horses or tough men, men like the Kileys. Maybe John Starr ...

Bright and warm, the May sunshine flooded the land. Only when a hatful of fleecy cloud now and again drifted across the sun did the faint chill in the air become noticeable. I dropped over the fence into the breaking corral, noticing that the fifty head or so in the big corral were spooky from being penned up. I signaled to Ox Pendroy to run in a batch of them.

The big man pushed the gate open, and he and Red Beckett choused half a dozen horses into the little corral. I shook out my loop, stealing a glance at the fence. The whole ranch was there, some of them, I knew, wanting to see me get piled. Mrs. Lowall and Sunny were seated on the top rail, with the two Kileys and a slim dark young fellow who must be Benton Lowall. Even Mrs. Ledger stood outside the gate, peering through the rails. I raised a hand in salute, not at all displeased at being the center of attraction. My attire of stag shirt, Levis, boots and batwing chaps didn't make much of a show, but I thought I managed a fine swagger as I moved toward the frightened horses.

good one. But at the end I was sitting him easily, jarred but still there. He didn't like it much.

Tired now, Reddy began to sulk. Then he thought of one more trick. He reared, trying to throw himself over backward, to crush this live thing on his back. I couldn't let him win that one, or he would be ruined. I didn't like to do it, but I let him have the butt of my quirt between his ears. He came down in a hurry, spinning. I belted him along the flanks, and went round the corral. Finally he quit cold. I hung the spurs into him and ran him until he was streaming with sweat. I could feel his muscles quivering under me, I stopped him then, swung on and off a dozen times. I kept patting him gently, talking to him.

When I stripped saddle, blanket, and bridle off him he stood stock still. Ox opened the gate to the big corral, but Reddy didn't come to life until Red Beckett ran at him, waving his arms. Then the horse spooked and trotted off into the wider reaches of the corral.

Mrs. Lowall came down from the high bars and hurried toward me.

"Very good, Tod; first rate. You weren't cruel, but you let him know who was boss. You keep your promises."

"I try to, Mrs. Lowall. I never baked a bronc yet, and I don't intend to start with your string," I told her.

"These are good horses, Tod. I'm sure you wouldn't ruin one." She glanced at the rail riders. "As some people might do."

Smiling, she walked back to Sunny. I walked over and got the stoneware jug out of the shade. I rinsed my mouth with the cool water and spat into the dust. I corked the jug and put it back.

Bent Lowall was looking over into the big corral, where the sweaty, dust-plastered Reddy was telling all about it to the sleek unridden horses. Then Lowall looked down at me. "Hell of a way to gentle a horse," he said.

"Gentle a horse?" I asked, surprised. "Kid, I didn't come to Lazy L to gentle horses. Your mother is paying me to break them. You pay for my time and patience, I can give you gentle horses. But I agree with your mother when she says there's no use putting a ten-dollar finish on a thirty-dollar horse. Tell you what I'll do, though. You pick out any one of these critters, and as a favor to you I'll train him so in two weeks he'll be following you around like a dog."

"I'll train my own horses," he said curtly. Young Kiley laughed. I turned toward him. I hadn't tangled with him since he hit the ranch a couple days ago, but I was willing. He must have known it, for he snarled silently at me and jumped down from the fence.

"C'mon, Bent, let's get out of here," he said.

"But I—" Bent began a protest.

"Damn it, come on," Shan Kiley said, and headed for the barn. Bent Lowall dropped from the fence and followed him.

A little later Rance Kiley gave me a sour look and went after them. I saw the three of them riding north. Good riddance, I thought, and went on about my horse business.

That afternoon Sunny was the lone spectator when I topped off my sixth bronc and decided to call it a day. I was stiff and sore, with the sensation that none of my joints would quite make connections. I knew it would ease up tomorrow, or I'd have quit. Just soft from lack of work, I decided.

I was taking a long swig of water from the stoneware jug when the girl came up beside me. When I was through she held out her hand for the jug, and I gave it to her. She tilted it up with an elbow as expertly as any old hand. As she drank, I could see the swell of her Adam's apple move in her long smooth throat. She put the jug down and drove the cork in with the heel of her hand.

"That was good," she said. "Tod, will you do me a favor? Mother said this spring I could have my pick of the range horses for a saddler. Will you gentle a horse for me?"

"Be happy to, Miss Sunny," I said. And meant it.

SIX

O N MOST ranches Sunday was just another day. But not on Lazy L. Mrs. Lowall insisted that Sunday be what the good Lord intended it to be, a day of rest. My first Sunday on the ranch I sure enjoyed sleeping in, for my muscles were still sore and stiff, though not as bad as the first day I started busting the Lazy L herd.

The sun was high when I finally rolled out. I washed and shaved and dressed. Then I meandered up to the big house to see if I could talk breakfast out of Mrs. Ledger. She gave me a long-suffering look. I gave her back a grin. Though her face was stern and grim, she reached over to the sideboard for the batter bowl. Before I knew it I was stowing away great golden hotcakes, sided with crisp bacon and two-three fresh eggs sunny side up. And drinking coffee as black as sin and as hot as a branding fire.

"Mrs. Ledger, I thought my maw was a good cook, and she was," I said, watching her spoon more batter onto the griddle. "But with all respect to her, God rest her, she wasn't in the same county with you when it comes to hotcakes."

Color touched her leathery cheeks. She set the bowl down with a thud. "You ain't going to get anywhere with all that soft soap," she said, her lips pursed. "Jest for that palaver, you can watch these cakes and flip 'em yourself. There's more coffee in the pot. Now I got beds to make and dustin' to do." She wiped her hands on her apron and left the kitchen.

I've fried a mort of flapjacks in my time. I was at the range watching them turn golden brown, when Sunny came in. She stopped in astonishment.

"I declare, we have a new cook! Good sir, prepare for me a bait of peacock's tongues on toast, and ambrosia to go with it."

"I'll fry you hotcakes," I said, digging a fresh plate, cup and saucer out of the cupboard. I poured coffee for her. "Sorry, peacocks are out of season, but Mrs. Ledger's coffee is the next best thing to the nectar of the gods."

She sat down. "Dear me, an educated horse wrangler," she said, reaching for cream and sugar. "What are you, Tod Morgan? A remittance man from the East?"

I filled my plate, pushed the griddle to the back of the stove, and took my place at the table. I reached out and speared a strip of bacon.

"No such luck," I told her. "I've always had to work for my bread and beans. I'm just a Kansas plowboy with mud on his boots, busting broncs for a hard living. Ten-fifteen years, I'll be stove up and crook-legged and full of rheumatiz. But right now it pays better'n tophand wages, so I'm giving it a whirl."

She looked me square in the eye. "You ever hire out that fast gun of yours?"

"Here and there," I said. I forked the last of the hotcakes into a stack, drowned them in a lick, and started in on them.

"My, you do talk a blue streak, Morgan," she said. She rolled the linen napkin and slid it into her silver ring. With exaggerated casualness she asked: "And what will you do after all that food, take a nap? Or would you be interested in seeing some of the country?"

I mopped my plate with the last of the hotcake and leaned back. "Darned near foundered myself," I said. "That nap, now. Sounds like a skookum idea."

"All right, my Siwash friend. Go sleep away the day, see if I care."

"Now that I think of it, I'm more of a Blackfoot. Got to wash up some socks and my other shirt, before it walks away."

"Lazy L is a civilized ranch," she said. "Bring your clothes here, and Mrs. Ledger will do them with the family wash. Now, with that taken care of, will you ride with me?"

"It would pleasure me, ma'am," I said. "Where to?"

She shrugged. "Oh, I don't know. Just out and away. But Mother won't let me ride alone. This is—well, a tough country."

"Pretty salty at that, from what I've seen. How about your beau, Shan Kiley? Won't he object?"

"Tod Morgan, Shan is not my beau. Maybe he'd like to be. But I ride with who I please!"

"The word is 'whom,' I think," I said with a grin. "All right, you get your riding duds on, and we'll go."

She jumped to her feet. "Saddle Mom's mare, will you? I'll be back in a jiffy."

Her "jiffy," of course, stretched to half an hour. Yet it was worth it. As we rode out the north gate and splashed through the swift waters of the ford, I watched her admiringly. Her riding habit was of a green whipcord, with silver piping and big silver buttons. With it she wore a saucy round hat like a derby. She made a pretty picture as she sat the sidesaddle on her mother's chestnut horse, in perfect ease and confidence.

Clear of the ranch fences, I asked, "Which way?"

"Would you like to see the Big River?"

"The Missouri? Sure, if only to prove to myself there's enough water somewhere in this country to float a steamboat."

"Precious few steamboats on this upper river now, since the N.P. built through. We might see one, though. How about going to Burnt Rock?"

"A trading post, isn't it? All right with me, if you say so. You know the trail?"

"I've been there," she said. "My brother Bent hangs out there a lot. Too much, I think. And, Tod, mind your step when we reach the post. Some of the men around there have bad reputations."

"That so?" I asked casually. "No need to worry, Miss Sunny. I'm a most peaceable man. I hate trouble."

"I'll bet!" she cried. "A real namby-pamby, with a hogleg .44 in your holster and a Winchester in the saddle boot. Don't josh me, Tod Morgan!"

She turned the chestnut into the north trail and led the way at a smart pace. This, I thought, is a lucky break. No need to make excuses now to look over the layout at Burnt Rock. I'd have an opportunity to see the center of outlaw activity for myself. I kept close track of the direction of the trail and the junctions. If Burnt Rock were the hornets' nest John Starr claimed it was, such knowledge might mean lives saved along the turns and ridges of the trail.

The country grew rougher. The basin where Lazy L dropped behind us. Deep coulees cut through the meager soil. Cutbanks loomed raw and white above the road. The vegetation was sparser here. The soil was yellow and gravelly, with a thin cover of gray sage and prickly pear. Among the ridges I saw the green of chokcherry and serviceberry, and an occasional twisted juniper. Dropping down toward the breaks of the river bottom, Sunny threaded her way carefully, for the trail was not much more than wash rock and old hoofmarks.

After a long flat rimmed with cottonwoods, the trail eased and turned east. Far to my left I caught a silvery glint that must be Missouri water. Not for several miles did trail and water converge, but at last we were on its bank. We stopped to give the horses a breather.

"Don't look like much," I said, a little disappointed. In truth, it seemed little greater than the Yellowstone. It was high now, from the spring thaws and rains, tawny-dark from the burden of silt it was carrying.

"Just you wait," Sunny said. She watched the stream intently. "There—look there!" she said, pointing.

Sailing down the back of the current came a big cottonwood log, majestic as a ship, but traveling like an express train. It drove along half submerged, slid into the narrow channel in front of us where a smaller log had lodged across the stream. The big floater hit it with a grinding crunch, and the smaller tree broke into bits. The chunks hung with the big tree as it sailed downstream, and in moments the whole raft was gone around a bend.

"Man, that's powerful water," I said. "I'd hate to try to ford it."

"Best not try it this time of year," Sunny said. "Even the ford at Burnt Rock is dangerous now. And it's best on the river for many miles."

Burnt Rock was five miles farther, through low ground choked with brush and cut by backwaters and sloughs. We came out on a rise above the post. It was a typical frontier settlement—large store, miscellaneous cabins and sheds, several tents half-sided with boards, the canvas dark with smoke and weather, a big corral. There were forty or fifty head of horses in the corral.

Sunny frowned when she saw them. She tossed me a glance of warning and led the way down into the settlement. I checked my guns and followed her.

A man was sitting in the shade at the front of the store. He let his chair tip forward, came to his feet, and stood waiting for us. As Sunny rode up, he shoved the hat back on his head with an insolent gesture and caught the cheekstrap of Sunny's horse.

"Well, sweetheart, you finally decided to honor Burnt Rock with your presence. And who's your rough, tough, hard-to-curry friend, here?"

"Let go of my bridle. This is Tod Morgan. Are you still running Burnt Rock with an iron hand, Ingersoll?"

"It runs itself," he said, I thought a little sourly.

Because a man's hands are sometimes a giveaway, I reached down from the saddle, offering Ingersoll a handshake. He met it with an air of surprise. His grasp was firm and brisk. He grinned up at me, a lean, wolfish grin that went part and parcel with his rangy build. I saw that he had a hard blue eye and a flash of gold in one front tooth. By the look of him he was whang leather and baleen, and could go round and round all day. A man to watch.

Sunny said, "We thought Bent might be here, Ingersoll."

"He is, down at the far corral," Ingersoll said. He gave her an odd warning look. "I wouldn't go down there, I was you."

Sunny, I had learned, bristled when she was opposed.

"Why not?" she asked.

As Ingersoll cocked his head, our answer came from beyond the store: a high keening scream, a shriek wrenched from the very vitals of a human being. The short hair stood up on the nape of my neck. The scream died to a whimper, and stopped.

"In the name of God, what was that?" I asked. I saw that Sunny's face had gone pale with shock.

Ingersoll shook his head, spat in distaste. "The boys caught a young Piegan buck trying to rustle horses early this morning. They're having a little fun with him before they hang him."

"Why don't you stop them?" Sunny asked indignantly.

"Miss Lowall, in this country a man lives longer if he minds his own business. Which is what I'm doing, though I'll admit I have no use for what they're pulling off. If you want to stop it, go ahead."

"And don't you think I won't!" Sunny cried. She spurred her horse into a dead run, heading for the corral. I followed her.

Half a dozen men were gathered in a knot in front of the rails. A small fire smoldered nearby. I saw Sunny slide from her horse and run toward the men, the fullness of her riding skirt caught in her hand. I jumped down from Prince and followed her. More slowly, though, for I was wary. I saw the men break away a little from the fence at her approach. Sunny screamed.

The object sagging in bonds from the corral rails might have been, early this morning, a man. Now it was a bloated caricature, the hawk face dropped down on the straining naked chest, the wire-coarse hair frizzed and scorched, one arm broken and dangling. Burned in the corded muscle of the coppery chest was a great XT. From a bullet hole in one thigh blood seeped to add to a dark pool on the ground. The face came up in a gasp for air. I saw that one eye had been torn out.

"You fiends! You rotten stinking beasts!" Sunny screamed. She ran toward the Indian. Shan Kiley, grinning blocked her way.

"Here, Bent, get her out of the way," he said.

Benton Lowall, with a sick look, came forward to take his sister's arm and pulled her away.

A giant of a man, with the dished face that denoted some Indian blood of his own, stirred up the fire. He looked at me, beads of sweat on his upper lip, an air of absorbed cruelty on him. "Stick around and watch the fun, brother," he said. "We're going to put our brand on his backside next. Hey, boys?"

"Dam' right," a tall skinny man said, spitting. "We'll teach these Blackfeet to rustle our hosses. We'll make this un screech some before we're through with him."

I walked closer. "You caught him red-handed, did you?"

The big man guffawed. "Well, sir, seein' as he's an Injun, wasn't much other way we could ketch him, was they? But you mean was he stealin' of our horses, he surer'n hell was. But what's your put-in here anyhow, sonny boy?"

"I just wondered," I said mildly. But inside, black-rage was tearing at me. I stood in front of the Indian.

The young Piegan's one good eye came open. A bright spark of understanding bridged the space between us. His gaze flickered for a split second to the gun at my side. I nodded.

"You did steal their horses, then?" I asked him.

"I stealum," he said in a rasping whisper. "Me, Pretty Wolf, fine good horse thief. Count coup many time. I stealum." Drained by the effort, he let his head drop forward on his chest.

My heart swelled with admiration for the supreme courage of this savage, and for his spirit under the awful torture these men had wrought on him. I showed it the best I knew how.

Deliberately, I drew my pistol and shot the Piegan through the heart.

"What the hell's the matter with you, you fool?" the big man yelled, springing toward me. I took a step to the side and laid the barrel of the Colt's alongside his temple with a full swing of my arm. He crumpled, falling as a tree falls. I stepped back to cover the rest.

Kiley had grabbed the girl. He tried to manhandle her, but she twisted with pantherish strength.

"Let her go, man," I said coldly. She broke away and got behind me.

"Young Lowall, get your horse," I said. Looking sick and scared, he walked away. I held the others under my gun.

"No matter if that Indian stole ten thousand horses," I told the five, "he didn't deserve such brutality. I hope you're proud of what you did this day to a man far braver than you'll ever be. I hope he haunts your sleep and your dreams. And for what you made me do to him, I'll pay you all one day, and double-measure."

I jammed the pistol back into the leather. I stood there, daring them, hoping one of them would make a break. But no one moved except the big man on the ground, who rocked and moaned, holding his head in his hands.

"Bring the horses up, Sunny," I told her.

Shan Kiley finally gathered his nerve. "You'll wish to hell you never saw Burnt Rock," he said.

"I already do," I said grimly. I took the reins from Sunny and mounted my horse. "And, Kiley, you're going to prod me once too often, one of these days. You won't have time to regret it."

Ingersoll stood on the porch in front of the store, whittling. As we rode around the corner of the building, he tossed the stick away, snapped his knife closed, and walked toward us.

"You've got plenty of insides, boy; I'll say that for you. And maybe an Injun friend among the Wolf People. I'm with you on what you did; the boys were going too dam' far. But they won't like you for it. Better not come back to Burnt Rock."

I leaned forward in the saddle. I said with deadly slowness: "Ingersoll, I'll come and go exactly as I please. I'm like that, and if any of these hardcase bullies want to stand in my way they're welcome to try. I'd just as soon gun them as not, after what I saw them doing today."

He gave me a long, hard look, that had a certain admiration in it. Then, without a word, he turned away and went inside the building.

We rode up the slant of the trail at a fast trot, without looking back. On top of the hill, Bent Lowall spurred his horse hard and went away from us, heading southwest at a fast pace. We followed more slowly.

Sunny rode with her head down, her shoulders slumped. Finally she gave a long shuddering sigh and straightened up. She turned to me.

"You made enemies today, Tod," she said.

"Who would want to call those devils friends?" I countered.

"They *are* devils," she admitted. "I hope this day was a lesson to my brother. He thinks the sun rises and sets in men like Shan Kiley and Jumbo Eiler and Art Cobb. The things they had done to that poor savage—Tod, it makes me sick to think of it. But was it right—the way you killed him?"

"What other way out was there for him? Or for me?"

She gave me a long, questioning look, shook her head, and was silent.

I was as silent, and I believe just as sick at heart, all the long road back to Lazy L.

SEVEN

I N THE WEEKS that followed, I settled into a routine so dull that I wondered sometimes if I was a lawman or a permanent bronc snapper. I had some relief when the spring rains turned the gumbo into a bottomless mire. Books could get tiresome too, I found, and checkers in the bunkhouse when the dripping gray skies blotted out the sun. I braided Sunny a fancy quirt, and set silver conchas on her best saddle. And answered her questions. I was more than pleased when the blaze of sun changed the gumbo into hardpan, and Red Beckett helped me rope the first horse into the breaking pen.

By now I hardly noticed the horse's color or the look in his eye. I got a hull onto him, let go his ear and rode him to a standstill. When I turned him loose, Ox Pendroy would make another mark in his tally book, and Red would cut out another victim.

A few days later I would take the same broomtails and give them three or four rides across the flats, with Ox or Red riding hazer alongside. After that, and a slicker lesson or two, I'd mark the horse graduated. It was tough work, brutal, monotonous work. I was getting plumb sick and tired of it.

I would have welcomed trouble with the Kileys: with Shan because the memory of the Indian, Pretty Wolf, still stuck in my craw and bothered my sleep at night; with Rance because I had him pegged now as a lowdown thief that was picking on a widow woman and her daughter. Nothing I saw gave me any proof of this; but by now, I thought, I could spot a badman at half a mile. And Rance Kiley was bad, all bad. Like a carcajou or a rattlesnake. There were straws in the wind that pointed to Rance being the big wheel in the stolen-horse trade, though so far he was too slick for me to pin a thing on him. But the time would come. He still pretended an interest in the horse breaking, and would show up at the corral several times a day, giving me his fishy eye. Shan, though, laid low.

So it was a surprise when Shan Kiley came riding up late one afternoon on a sleek bay horse with the big Lazy L on its left hip. He was leading a nondescript gray with a blocky conformation and a sleepy eye. I watched Kiley, wary. Out of the corner of my eye I caught a glimpse of Sunny Lowall hurrying down from the house.

I stood there, sucking on a quirley, waiting for him. He tied his horse, and came into the corral on foot, leading the gray. He shoved his hat back on his head and grinned at me.

"Morgan, I guess I got off on the wrong foot," he said. "I didn't want to have no hand in mistreating that Injun, but I should have stopped the boys from doing it. I been thinkin', you done the right thing when you shot him." He put out a hand.

I shook it, taken by surprise and the sudden fairness of his words.

"To hang a thief is one thing, Kiley," I said. "To torture a man, red or white, is another. Best we all forget it."

"Good," he said. "Because I want a favor from you. Slim Ingersoll, down to the Burnt Rock store, sold me this critter cheap. He's been hoorawed one time; he's spooky. But I got a hunch he's got good stuff in him. You think you could make a cow pony out of him?"

I didn't like the Roman nose on the horse, but Kiley had me fair treed.

"Cost you ten dollars, Kiley, and even then I can't guarantee results."

He dug down in his pocket and came up with a gold eagle. "Here you are. I'll be 'way ahead of Ingersoll if you can make something out of this broomtail."

Shan Kiley bearing gifts was enough to make me wary. The gray didn't fight blanket or saddle, nor did he fight the curb bit I slipped into his mouth. As I swung into the saddle and settled myself firmly, I noticed Ox, Red, and Sunny Lowall all take to the high rail. Shan Kiley, though, still stood close to the gray's off side. He pulled something from his pocket.

Before I could make a move, he had thrown a loop of tough buckskin around my ankle and stirrup and pulled it tight. He stepped back, drawing his pistol. He fired it under the gray's belly so close it must have scorched the hide.

I didn't have time to wonder. The gray flew all apart. He was a goer; he felt like spring steel and gutta-percha. He was wound up like an eight-day clock. It took only one jump to tell me he was an outlaw. From there on in, he opened up a bag of tricks the like of which I never hope to see again. He had me weaving like beargrass in a windstorm. But I slammed my spurs into his shoulders, raking the rowels across the gray hide.

When he reared to throw himself backward, I felt panic surge up in me, knowing why Shan Kiley had tied my foot into the iron. I had no quirt, but I smashed the gray between the ears with my clenched fist, He squalled, and came back to earth. He bolted once around the corral. On the second round Kiley swung the gate of the corral open. The gray rocketed through. In the open, he laid his belly to the ground and ran.

A bronc can, and does, run crazy blind. That's why we run them with a flanker riding alongside to turn them. There was nobody to turn this one. He lit out through the sagebrush, his head down, not knowing or caring where he was going. It didn't matter a whit that there was a deep coulee cutting the flat in front of us, nor that he was heading hellbent for it.

I laid into the brute, hauling and raking, and all the time cursing Shan Kiley for a tricky no-good. I pulled leather, and leaned out to my right. I managed to get the loop of the rawhide thong in my fingers. I pulled on it with a hard, steady pressure. At the last moment the rawhide stretched and the knot slipped free. We were right at the edge of the wash.

With hands and knees and voice I tried to lift the gray over the wash. It was just too wide. He hit on the far bank, his feet bunched like a cat's. He almost made it, but he was going too fast. As he lurched, I kicked my feet free and unloaded. I lit running, took half a dozen giant steps before I lost my balance. I rolled through the sage, dry stems crackling, twigs gouging my face and hands. When I stopped, I lay still for a minute. I worked arms and legs. They seemed intact. I rubbed the blood from a torn cheek and stood up. I limped back.

The gray was there, his legs all awry, his neck at an impossible angle. He was dead. Looking at him, I felt a pang of pity for the beast. He had fought his best, without fear or malice. Here was another count against Shan Kiley.

My saddle was such a wreck, the tree broken, the horn bent, the leather slashed and ripped, that I didn't bother to take it off. I climbed down into the coulee and up the other side. I started to walk toward Lazy L, astonished that we had traveled so far away from it.

Hoofs pounded, and Sunny came racing up on Ox Pendroy's cutting horse. She was riding like an Indian woman, astride, her skirt hiked shamelessly high about long, beautiful legs.

"Tod! Tod! Are you hurt?" she cried.

"Half killed, but I'll make 'er," I told her. I reached up my arms. "Get down here, kid. You're making a holy show of yourself."

"Who's to see but you?" she asked pertly. But she slid down from the horse into my arms. I felt the vibrant, yielding warmth of her for just a moment. Then I released her.

"I'll take the horse," I said.

She handed me the reins. "Why do you want him?"

"So I can ride down Shan Kiley and shoot him to death," I said.

"No, Tod, please!" she cried, throwing herself against me. "He's gone now. It would mean trouble, bad trouble. For our sake, Mother's and mine, let him go! Tod, the right day will come."

I had a hand on the horn, ready to mount, when her words stopped me cold. If I went after Kiley, the resulting showdown would make me useless for the job John Starr had given me. The job was bigger than I was. Sunny was right; there would be a reckoning later. But in my own time—and Starr's.

But I was sore. "All right, if he means so much to you I'll let him go," I said, just for the sake of hurting something.

Tears came to her eyes. "Not for my sake," she said. "For yours, Tod. He hoped the gray would hurt you. But he knew that if you escaped you would get mad, Tod, just as you have. He knew that if you rode into Burnt Rock after him, you'd find Eiler and Art Cobb and the Daylight Kid and others with ready guns. They'd cut you down and laugh about it."

"How do you know so much?" I demanded, still riled up.

"I haven't lived on the same ranch with Shan Kiley for nothing. And gone to school with him, until he dropped out. And watched him and listened to his brag. Tod, Shan is wily and dangerous, but I can read him like an open book."

With gentle fingers she touched my torn cheek and gave me such a brilliant, warming smile that I could only melt. I put my hands under her arms and boosted her not inconsiderable weight to a seat in front of the saddle. I swung up and steadied her with an arm.

As we rode off, I said, "This is the first ride we've had together since Burnt Rock."

"Tod, I should have told you. Burnt Rock was out of bounds for me when we went there. Mother heard of the doings, of the killing of that poor Indian boy, and she limited me to the ranch for three weeks. My time was up today."

"You had it coming," I told her. But I couldn't feel very angry about it. "How about your brother?" I headed the horse toward the ranch.

"Oh, he's back to normal. He was mighty subdued for a few days, but he's back in the old braggart ways, hanging around Burnt Rock, listening to the wild tales of those renegades. Tod, I'm afraid of them. They'll lead Bent into terrible trouble. He's not bad, Tod. He's just full of romantic tales and half-digested theories."

"Sunny, for your mother's sake, get him away from that outfit," I said, going as far as I could by way of warning.

At the corral, I dismounted. Sunny slid into my arms, the litheness of her body against me sending a shock through me. She whirled lightly away and ran toward the house.

"Nice ride, Tod," Ox Pendroy said, smirking. He took the reins of his horse.

"Go to hell!" I told him. But I had to grin at the big oaf.

Down at the bunkhouse, I cleaned up with strong soap and warm water. I put on fresh duds, taking my sweet time. For I had seen the horse tied at the rail in front of the house.

It was Roller. John Starr was here.

EIGHT

"MR. STRATTON, meet our bronc breaker, Tod Morgan," Beth Lowall said. "Tod, treat Mr. Stratton well. He might be one of our best customers. He's a remount buyer for the British cavalry."

"Pleased to know you, Stratton," I said, shaking hands with my uncle as solemnly as if I had never seen him before in my life.

"How do, Morgan," he said. "Mrs. Lowall tells me you're a top hand with horses. I'm sure she wouldn't mind if you check through the herd with me when I come to purchase."

"Lazy L won't get any the worst of my opinion," I warned.

Starr laughed. "Oh, I would expect that, and discount it."

"Tod wouldn't lie about our horses," Sunny said indignantly.

"Why, I'm sure he wouldn't, Miss Lowall," Starr said with deference. "I shouldn't be facetious about a matter like that. My apologies."

"Don't get ory-eyed, Sunny," I added. "My opinion would only be a courtesy. If Mr. Stratton couldn't cull a horse herd with about a ten-second glance at each animal, he wouldn't be a remount buyer."

"Modesty dictates that I should deny that," he said, smiling. "But then word might get around that I was an easy mark, which would result in a waste of my time and the British Government's. For even with the pick of your fine herd, Mrs. Lowall, I'll have to scour the country to fill the order I have in hand. Because the horses I buy must be hardy brutes, sound of wind and limb, and meeting certain specifications of size and weight."

Benton Lowall was sprawling on the settee, the usual glum disinterest on his narrow face. Now he perked up, straightened, and leaned forward toward Starr. "How many head can you use, Stratton, on top of what Lazy L can furnish?"

"Why, five hundred head as a minimum. A thousand, and I wouldn't have to make my Wyoming trip. Next year the same. Why, have you something in mind?"

Lowall stood up and came over, shouldering me and Starr. There was a stink of horse and sweat and buckskin and stale smoke about him. I'm no prairie flower, but I stepped back. My uncle merely smiled.

"You mean business?" Bent demanded excitedly, as if ideas were crowding him too fast to be sorted out.

Starr stared at him with some asperity, and without answering.

"Well, I just meant—hell, Stratton, this is a big deal. I'd go to a lot of trouble to set it up. The pay would have to be in cash. And I'd want my share."

"Since you question the integrity of Her Majesty's Government, we will certainly make it cash," Starr said. "And you are, of course, entitled to a legitimate commission. Where will you get these horses?"

"Never mind that," Bent said arrogantly. "That's where I'll make my commission." He stood up and grabbed his hat.

"Where are you going, Benton?" his mother asked.

"To Burnt Rock."

"Isn't it—rather late?"

"Listen, Beth, I'm not a kid any more. I come and go as I please, like every man does. I said I was going to Burnt Rock." He headed for the door.

"One minute, Lowall." Starr's voice was cold.

Benton stopped, and turned his head.

"You didn't ask about one factor that might affect your plans. These horses you say you can supply—they must be gathered and ready to trail to the railroad by the middle of July. My employers want the sea passage made in good weather."

"They'll be ready," Bent said, and went out.

After supper, a meal made more pleasant by the absence of Benton Lowall, we gathered in the big living room. After asking Mrs. Lowall's permission, Starr lit one of his slim Havana cigars.

"A fine broad country, this Montana Territory," he said through the drift of tobacco smoke.

"Your first time here, Mr. Stratton?" Beth asked.

He nodded. "But I like it. Plenty of room in it."

"Plenty of hidey-holes for outlaws, too," Sunny said.

"I hear that they are quite strong, and a very disturbing element, Miss Lowall. But that will pass, as the tide of civilization flows west."

"It had better bring some law with it, then," Sunny said. "I'm sick and tired of roughnecks and renegades and criminals. That's all the kind I ever meet, seems to me. Except for you, Tod, and Mr. Stratton. Why, right on Lazy L, that Shan Kiley! What that precious brother of mine sees—"

"Sunny!" Her mother cut her off.

"Well, Mother, after that dreadful torture of the Indian, and then what Shan pulled off this afternoon ..."

She recounted the deadly trick Kiley had tried to work on me with the outlaw gray. "Mother," she concluded indignantly, "we've got to get rid of those Kileys. Both of them."

"I know, I know," Beth said resignedly. "But give me time, my dear. There are things you don't understand."

"I understand, all right. You're afraid of Rance Kiley! Well, I'm not, and one of these days I'm going to run him off Lazy L with a shotgun. He hasn't any more claim to part of the ranch than—than Mr. Stratton here!"

"Sunny, you're just a child," her mother said. "You must let me work these things out in my own way. Do you think it's of my own choice that I defer to Rance Kiley? Or care for his son, with his unhealthy influence on Benton?"

"I heard about the Indian, Morgan," Starr said to me. "In the code of the frontier, he was their prisoner. But, in interfering, I believe you acted according to your rights."

"The Indian was a human being," I said stiffly. "Not even a low cur ought to be treated as they treated him. There was no possibility of his living. I set him free. And I'd do the same again."

"Good for you, young man," Starr said, rising. "Mrs. Lowall, could I persuade you to join me in a stroll, after that fine meal?"

As she rose, smiling to join him, I was astonished to see a surprising softness in my uncle's usually taciturn face. Could Beth Lowall, I wondered, bring about such a change in a man?

"I've set out the bait, by way of Benton Lowall. Now let us see if the fish will rise to it," Starr said.

Our horses were cropping new grass a few yards away, while we sat in the spring sunlight on a rise overlooking Elk Creek. Below us at the base of a sheer cutbank flowed the swollen yellow creek. To the north the country ran far away into the blue-hazed distances beyond the Missouri. The air was crystal. We could see the slashed and twisted land, the winding coulees, the willow-greened courses of all the little creeks and runs. In the vast emptiness of the landscape, only a herd of cattle moved, grazing on a ridge in the middle distance and looking like children's toys.

"They might be suspicious," I said.

"They're always that, Tod. But the yellow gleam of a double-eagle will blind them to common sense. This rabble is always the same, boy. Greed makes them predictable. They'll be no question of my good faith when they hear the clink of coin. No, Tod, they'll take the hook, and the line and sinker as well."

"If they find you out, you're dead," I warned him.

He laughed. "All life is played at long odds, Tod. I'll bet high to get a crack at these renegades. Grant Stevens has shown me some of the material he has gathered through agents working as we are. This is a tough, vicious gang. If they aren't stopped—and soon—they'll rule and ruin this rich land."

"They're tough enough, God knows," I said, the memory of Pretty Wolf still strong in me.

"They'll tame, Tod, tame or die," he said, his fingers touching his pistol butt. "You have any results to report at Lazy L?"

"Results?" I asked testily. "I've got calluses on my rump like horn buttons, from snapping broncs. But daggone little information. No sign that Mrs. Lowall and the girl are anything but honest horse raisers. The two hands, Pendroy and Beckett, are good men, top hands, but they keep their mouths tight closed. I can't pump a thing out of them. Young Lowall is a reckless fool, just as his pa, Tall Tom Lowall, was a reckless fool before him. The Kileys, father and son, are up to their butts in plenty of deviltry. They are away from Lazy L most of the time, but I think they're tolling Bent Lowall into their schemes to get their hooks into the ranch. I'm hoping Mrs. Lowall proves too smart for them."

"Kiley must be a home-grown badman. They're often the worst kind. He's on my list."

"Better watch him, then. He has that wild, mean look about him, and he fancies himself chain lightning with a six-gun."

"Is he?"

"I beat him."

"Still might be pretty good," John Starr said.

I grinned acknowledgment of the compliment.

"Tod," my uncle went on, "things will start to move now. Bent Lowall has his eye on that commission. The big man, or men, will get the word. And the thieving will start, all along the underground road. That's why I made the bait big, so that they would bet the stack. In addition, the open rustling will antagonize the remaining ranchers who have been lukewarm toward Grant Stevens and the other leaders."

"Think there is a leader to the ring?" I asked.

"That's hard to say. It may be a loose setup with three or four men running the show. Or it might be that the ring is under the thumb of one man. Such as Ingersoll at Burnt Rock."

"Or Rance Kiley."

"Or Rance Kiley. Tod, Kiley is your job. Is there any chance Lazy L might be a way station, or interchange point, on the underground?"

I shook my head. "Not with the four honest souls I mentioned before. Burnt Rock would be more likely. All the stock I've worked, at Lazy L, has been clean. I'm sure of that. You and Stevens are certain there is such a secret trail?"

"Positive. We know it stretches from Fort Calgary clear down into the Nations. It's big business, Tod; and so far it's been as safe as houses for the men running it. We hope to change that."

As we rode back toward the ranch, I said: "All right, I'll try to find out where Kiley goes and what he does. But more than likely I'll get my head blown off my shoulders. Still, that might be better'n stomping broncs six days a week forever. So I'll try to track him—if I can get away from that kid Sunny long enough."

"You want to dodge Sunny like a bear wants to dodge a bee tree," my uncle said. "And I can't say I blame you."

The next day my uncle rode away to the west, and I went back to the grinding routine of topping broncs. It gave me plenty of time to study the Kileys.

I discovered that they didn't miss much that went on at the ranch. Rance would always check me out at the corral if he was leaving, or else Shan Kiley would be hanging around, with his fishy eye on me. He steered wide of me, though. I had beaten the living daylights out of him the first time I caught him after the killer-horse episode. Pretty fair fighter, Shan was. I had a beautiful mouse on my right eye for a week.

But it was now mid-June, and time was running out. I grew a little desperate. Grant Stevens wanted proof, and I wasn't getting it for him. Grudgingly, I admitted to myself that getting proof was the just thing to do; our evidence had to be irrefutable.

"You may have to take chances, Tod," Starr had told me. "But remember, if you get caught, we'll have to disown you."

I had wanted to ask him about that, but just then Beth Lowall had come from the house, and Starr had forgotten me.

Now the rains were over. The grama and the buffalo grass were tinting the rolling slopes with yellow-green. Ox and Red took the wagon and went to Miles City for a load of bob-wire fencing and a night on the town. Bent Lowall and Shan Kiley had ridden off on one of their mysterious pasears early in the morning. And my shadow, Sunny, was visiting near neighbors at the Circle Star, twenty miles or so away. The place seemed strangely quiet.

The day was overcast and muggy, with the constant threat of rain in the air. Single-handed, I worked with some of the range horses I was giving the special treatment at Mrs. Lowall's request. I was tired when I came in to supper. Mrs. Ledger noticed it.

"Have another piece of pie, youngster," she said. "You cain't battle them jughaids all day 'thout puttin' back some o' that energy you burn up. Come on, now.

I didn't refuse, for the old girl was a marvelous cook.

"I can't say no," I told her. "But as soon as I'm through I'm heading for the bunkhouse. Dunno what's the matter with me, but I can't keep my eyes open."

"Maybe you read too late, Tod," Mrs. Lowall said gently. "You get a good night's sleep, you'll feel better tomorrow."

I saw Rance Kiley's cat's-eyes swing to me, yellow in the lamplight. I thought I saw a gleam of satisfaction in them.

"Spring fever, that's all the matter with you, young man," Mrs. Ledger said emphatically. "What you need is a good dose of sulphur and molasses. You jest wait one minute..."

I didn't wait. I grabbed the slab of pie in one hand and my Stetson in the other and like to busted the screen door wide open as I ducked out the back way, followed by the laughter of Mrs. Lowall and Mamie Ledger. Even Rance Kiley chuckled.

I stayed in the bunkhouse just long enough to bolt the pie, and darned good it was, too. Then I slid around behind the bunkhouse to the barn. As fast as I could work, I saddled Blackie, one of the Lazy L riding string. I led him out into the small corral and tied him up in the shadow of a hay shed. Then I headed back toward the bunkhouse on the dead run.

All I had to worry about now was Rance discovering my saddled horse when he left. And I did worry, all through the long slow twilight. Seemed like it would never get dark. The curtains stirred gently as the night breeze arose. Finally the lamps in the ranchhouse winked out. Things gave a final little stir and went quiet.

The light scrape of a bootsole jerked me out of a doze. I heard the gentle creak of the door opening. Against the faintly lighter rectangle of the door I could make out the loom of a man's body. Excitement rose in me. I found it hard to pretend sleep, and to keep my breathing slow and even. After two or three endless minutes I heard the door close softly. Footsteps, less careful now, receded across the hard-packed yard.

I lay still, taut as a snubbing line, until I heard the protest of wood on wood that was the corral gate being opened. I was wearing pants and boots under the blanket, so it took only a second to don shirt and vest, grab my hat, gunbelt, and rifle and ease out of the door.

The coin-yellow disk of the bright moon was just lifting out of the east. Its light was an eerie glow on grass and willow and sage. For just a moment a rider was outlined like a cardboard cutout against the yellow moon as he topped the rise on the east trail. Then he dipped over the hill and was gone.

I raced to the corral, buckling my gunbelt as I ran. I jammed the carbine into the saddle boot and jerked Blackie's reins loose from the rail. I mounted fast, the horse taking the open gate at a dead run. I didn't dare let Kiley get too great a lead, or he would be gone.

Night trailing, even in bright moonlight, is a tricky business. Light and shadow are deceptive, distances measureless. Sounds drift through the soft night air with startling clarity, but a man must guess at their point of origin. Starr had given me long, hard training in this as in other things. Yet if Rance had left the well worn trail, I would have lost him in the first ten minutes.

Seeing that he was heading toward Burnt Rock, I dropped back a little, close enough to catch a glimpse of his dark shape against the sky on the upgrades, and stopping to listen for the click and thud of hoof on gravel. I was lucky enough to catch the sound when he turned east off the main trail. I strained eyes and ears to locate him. I loosened my pistol in its holster and sent Blackie into the trail at a swifter pace.

The moon had gone high in a star-flecked sky and was flooding the land with pale light, yet Kiley still went on. Suddenly, I jerked Blackie up and clamped my fingers over his jaws. Ahead, at the peak of the rise, a rider had appeared, a silhouette against the glow of the sky.

"Rance! Rance! That you?" a voice called.

Ahead of me, Kiley yelled: "No names, damn you! Won't you ever learn common sense?"

NINE

Kᴉʟᴇʏ's ᴄʜᴀʟʟᴇɴɢᴇʀ laughed, a great booming gust of amusement. I knew him then—Jumbo Eiler, the big man I had laid out with a pistol barrel the day of Pretty Wolf's death.

"Sho, Kiley, ain't skeered, are you? We got this country by the tail on a down hill drag. Come on, the boys are waiting in the next coulee."

Kiley said something I didn't catch.

"Oh, fer God's sake it's only a little fire," Eiler said. "Art Cobb shot a antelope buck and we're cookin' some steaks. Come on, now, you don't get meat like that every day."

Kiley must have protested again.

"Aw, the hell with it! Ain't nobody going to be skyhootin' around in this brush all hours of the night. I'm hungry," Eiler told him.

I let them ride off, remembering Starr's words about the stupidity of such men. Though it might mean their lives, they would forego guard duty to stuff their bellies.

When I judged it safe, I tethered Blackie well off the trail. I noted a twisted juniper to mark the spot. Keeping low, I Injuned along through the rocks, watchful for men or rattlesnakes. The person who says that anybody, even an Indian, can move through brittle sagebrush by moonlight *without a sound* is a damned liar! But I kept as quiet as possible. Nor was it too risky, for animals both large and small prowl the range on moonlit nights

I was lucky, and the outlaws were careless. I caught the reflected flicker of the fire that Kiley had complained about, well before I reached the rim of the coulee. Wood smoke came pungent to my nostrils, and the fatty smell of frying meat. Crawling now, I found the rim. Below, the fire flared yellow in the black pit of the coulee. It was almost straight down, under a rocky cliff.

Some ten men sat or lolled in the firelight. A demijohn with a wicker cover was passing from hand to hand. As Eiler finished tying his horse to a bush, a man handed him the jug. He lifted it with elbow and forearm, his head tilted back. Finally he lowered it slowly. He stood for a long minute without moving a muscle. Then he shook himself like a wet dog. He stamped his feet on the ground in a little dance. With both hands he passed the jug along.

"Wahoo! That ain't good, but, 'fore God, she's got authority!" he said. "Where'd you get 'er? She didn't come from Ingersoll's. With his'n, your gizzard flops twice and settles back. Mine's still flutterin'!"

"Made 'er myself, Jumbo," a bearded man said. "That's Blackfoot trade whisky, the kind they run on the Whoop-Up Trail. Grain alkihall, cut with ditchwater and prune juice. I give 'er a cup of glycerine to the bar'l to make a bead, a plug of eatin' tobaccer for color, a handful of Cayenne to make 'er bite, and two, three rattlesnake heads in the bottom of the crock, jest on general principles. What do you think of 'er?"

"She's plumb hairy, Flicker," Eiler said. "After one drink I'm ready to hit the warpath."

"I'm giving you the chance, Jumbo," Rance Kiley said.

The roistering crew went silent. I could hear the snap and crackle of the fire, and the wail of a coyote in the dim distance.

"What you gettin' at, Rance?" Eiler asked, then.

"Just what I said. Tonight we clean out Silver Spring. It's time to shut Bart Stoker up. For keeps."

I clenched my fists until the knuckles hurt. In the weeks at Lazy L, I had learned to know the old storekeeper well, for he was a great friend of Beth and Sunny Lowall. These men were planning his death. I strained to catch every word.

"He's spying for the association," Kiley went on. "Passing names and movements along to the range detectives. Or so the word on the Injun telegraph says. I'm gonna make an example of him."

"Burn him out?"

"Burn him out—after we've lifted his cache and picked out the goods we want. I want him out of the way before next week."

"When we bring them horses down from Canada for that limey Stratton?" somebody asked.

"That's it. With the ones we have tagged around here, we can fill his order."

"Does he think we raise 'em?" a man asked, and laughed.

"Stratton's not a fool, Cobb. But he needs horses, and he ain't too dam' particular where they come from, if we don't overplay it. So Flicker—Flicker Hardy—don't you glom onto any critters with the Mounted Police brand burned into the hoof, or I'll skin you alive!"

"It was jest that onst, Rance," the bearded man protested. "I won't do it again."

The men hooted with laughter.

Kiley tucked the last chunk of greasy meat into his mouth and stood up, wiping his fingers on his dirty trousers. He took a swig from the demijohn, coughed, and drove the cork in with the heel of his hand.

"All right, boys," he said. "Get your tails into them saddles and we'll ride. We'll have Silver Spring cleaned out before sunup. Then we scatter and lay low. I want everybody to keep out of trouble until we meet at Burnt Rock on the fifth day of July. The big herd will come down out of Canada that day, near as I can figger. You'll have to help bring 'em across the river."

The men moved, picking up their gear. I gathered my knees under me, ready to crawl away. Then I heard Kiley and Jumbo Eiler talking below me.

"You shoulda got your boy Shan and the Lowall kid blooded tonight, Rance," Eiler said. "But I don't see them. They too pure to get blood on their fingers?"

"Bent Lowall's our contact with Stratton. I'm keeping him in the. clear for now. Shan's as wild as a loco wolf. I can't make him take orders, even if he is my own kid. So I don't want him around on a ticklish business like this. I swear, Jumbo, all that brat of mine can think of is gunning young Morgan."

"He'll play hell doin' it. That bronc snapper is pure poison. He's dam' sudden, and mean as they come. I know. Tell Shan to shinny on his own side; I'll take care of Morgan. But only when the signs are right—jest right."

"I thought mebbe he was a spy for the association. But he works too hard and carries too big a chip on his shoulder. I know dam' well he's on the dodge. Wisht we had him on our side."

"Yeah, Shan thinks *he's* a hardcase, but he ain't in it with Morgan. Lookit the way Morgan kilt that Injun, right under our guns. Oh, I'll take care of him, all right. But most likely with a Winchester, from a dry gulch, damn him!"

"You ain't bullin' for the little Lowall heifer, like Shan is, Jumbo?" Kiley asked with a laugh.

"Hell, no. But that ma of hers, now ..."

Kiley's voice went cold and hard. "I ever see you looking cross-wise toward Beth Lowall, Jumbo, I'll kill you."

"You got a claim staked?"

"You're damn' right I have. Why else do you think I paid to have Tall Tom killed in a Billings saloon?"

I watched them walk away. I was so startled by this information I almost forgot why I was there. I came alive abruptly, and eeled my way back from the rim of the cliff, knowing I had let my margin of time shrink far past the point of safety. I came to my feet and ran, regardless of noise, toward my tied horse. And had a moment of panic when he was not there. Then I heard a soft whicker. I hurried another fifty yards down the trail to find him tied by an almost identical juniper tree. I jerked the reins loose and mounted Blackie on the dead run, heading toward Silver Spring.

Even while I worried about Bart Stoker, and whether I could reach him through little known country before Kiley and his gang did, I was exultant about what I had learned, and even a little pleased with the reputation I seemed to hold among the outlaws. I wondered whether Beth Lowall suspected that her husband had been deliberately murdered by the man who professed to be his partner.

In any case I would have plenty to report to John Starr. I thought now of my uncle's attitude toward such men. Wolves killed because of hunger, but these men talked of robbery and treachery and murder as if it were the most natural thing in the world. Anger grew in me. Even without the memory of Mary Reade I could almost believe with John Starr that these lawless, Godless men must be exterminated as ruthlessly as calf-killing lobos.

We stormed across Elk Creek, the trail an inky tunnel through the giant cottonwoods. The horse grunted, climbing the steeps beyond Dry Wash. We drove down the far side, bright spray fanning like crystal beads in the moonlight as we galloped through the shallow ford of Lame Cow Creek. Then one final hill, and below me were the toy cubes of buildings, the Silver Spring store and post.

I pulled Blackie to a halt, looking for signs of life below. The immense silver flood of the moonlight laid everything out in clear white and jet shadow, picking out fence rail and chimney jack, and flashing from the glass panes at the front of the store as if from a mirror. The wagon track curved past into the gray-black sage, swinging up the hill to where I was. I spurred Blackie down its arc, but turned off behind the barn to tie him in the screen of the willows.

I caught my rifle in the crook of my arm, jumped the little runlet from the perpetual spring and, crouching low, ran toward the store. There was no sign of riders yet, and I breathed easier. I found a window partly open in the little cabin beside the store.

"Bartl Bart Stoker!" I called urgently.

Inside, bedsprings creaked. Someone grunted.

"Bart! Open up, for God's sake! There's trouble," I cried.

"What in tarnation ye want, this time o' night?" came the querulous old voice. "Who in Gehenna are ye?"

"Tod Morgan, Bart. Get your clothes on fast! The wild bunch is raiding you! Tonight."

"Sho! You don't say! Well, sir, wait until I get me a lantrun—"

"No, Bart, no! You've got to hurry! They know you've been working for Grant Stevens. They're out to kill you!"

The cabin door swung open on well oiled hinges. The old man stood there in a shaft of moonlight, ludicrous in baggy long underwear. But there wasn't anything funny about the Navy cap and ball he was aiming at me.

"By crimeny, it *is* Tod Morgan! Who are these men, Tod, that are after Bart Stoker's skelp?"

"Eiler, Hardy, Art Cobb, Joe, Bill, Tex, and half a dozen other hardcases. Names don't matter. Two of us can't stand them off. So get your valuables and we'll duck out."

Bart Stoker snorted. "Show you my cache? You think I'm tetched in the head? I'm stayin' right here."

This old fool will get us both killed, I thought in anger.

"You ornery old goat, get your pants on! You want to know, I'm a range detective, working for Grant Stevens. I'm telling you, Bart, we don't dig out of here pronto we're both dead men!"

"I declare, you *do* mean it, don't you?" He handed me his pistol and disappeared into the room. In two minutes he was back, fully dressed, a double-barreled shotgun in one hand, a small grip in the other.

"All right, Morgan, let's get on with it. Don't get no idears about this valise; it's jest got some personal things in it, and half a dozen boxes of ca'tridges. My real cache is back in the hills, and safe. I ain't no Johnny-come-lately in this country."

He slammed the door and locked it. We skinned out toward the creek. I stood guard while he got his best horse saddled and led him out to tie him beside Blackie, well away from the buildings. On foot, we moved back toward the barn.

We were lying in the safety of the willow screen when the outlaws came storming down the hill. They fanned out among the buildings, the soft light catching the gleam of gun barrels.

Bart Stoker winced as glass crashed. Something heavy tipped over inside the store. There was loud laughter until Kiley yelled from the porch: "Well, find him, damn you! He's here somewhere. Search every building. Bring him here to me."

Two men came down toward us.

Pinto tells me the old man had three or four good saddles," one of them said.

"Those I could use," the other said. "That old kack of mine is bust' down to scraps and splinters. Let's take a look."

Beside me, I heard the old man mutter darkly. I put a hand on his back, holding him flat.

"Hey, here's a lantern," one of them said from inside the door. "Gimme a match, Art."

"Tod, you got to stop him," Bart Stoker murmured. "That daggone lantrun's tricky. First thing you know, he'll …"

It was already too late. The match flared yellowly; the lantern wick caught. Jumbled shadows dipped and swayed in the open doorway. The light dimmed as they went deeper into the low building. Suddenly we heard a yelp of pain. The light swung in a wide arc. Glass crashed.

"Dang handle gets hot; then a man burns his fingers on the top." Bart Stoker explained. "Now he's dropped it. Look out, Tod!"

He tried to get up, but I held him hard. Inside the barn the light had turned from yellow to red. The dry hay and straw had caught. Coughing and wheezing, the two men stumbled from the barn.

"You clumsy jackass!" one of them said. "Look what you gone and done. And no saddles, either. Kiley won't like this."

"Hell with Kiley! He ain't tellin' me nothin'. C'mon, let's get these horses out of here. Let the old rat's nest burn."

The horses were plunging and neighing in panic as the flames mounted. The two men had to drag them by main force away from the burning building. Sparks soared and flared in the night sky as the men led the saddlers away.

Bart Stoker struggled against me as I dragged him to greater safety back in the brush. He was cursing steadily. When he reached the end of his devil's litany, he began over again. I had a hard time convincing myself that it would be sheer suicide for the two of us to show ourselves in front of a gang as tough as this one. I was mad enough to do it, and so was the old man; but even if we got a few of them, the rest would hunt us down like rabbits.

Now, as if sight of the flames had driven them to pure frenzy, the gang indulged in an orgy of destruction. They drove their horses, loaded with loot, away from the store and put the building to the torch. Glass smashed; stored ammunition popped off like firecrackers. Fire leaped from the roof of the cabin. A man came running with a great torch, tossed it into the chicken pens, and then stood there jumping up and down in crazy delight as the poor birds squawked in terror. He ran back, got another flaming brand, and hurled it into a sturdy lean-to alongside the store wall.

"That warn't so damn' smart, mister," Bart Stoker said, *sotto voce*. He knew what he was talking about. The lean-to erupted, and the earth bucked and rolled beneath us. The wall of the store surged and buckled inward. A man screamed in a long ululation of stark pain. The horses were going mad with fear.

In the blaze of light from the buildings, men went running. They mounted quickly, spurring their horses away. One man sagged limply in his saddle, another supporting him from the side. In little more than seconds, the yard was empty. The last rider went pounding over the hill, leaving us to face a scene of utter destruction.

Bart Stoker stood up stiffly. As I stood beside him I could feel him quivering. In the flickering light his old face was seamed and drawn.

"Wisht they'd got to my powder house quicker. Might of blowed the whole hellfire bunch to damnation, he said. He took a round can of snoose from his pocket. With careful deliberation he inserted a big pinch inside his lower lip. Then he spat.

"They didn't leave you much, Bart," I said.

"Not much. Though I've got a couple or three ounces of dust cached out, enough to rebuild. But what's the use? The murderin' devils will just come back again."

"I think, old-timer, their race is about run," I said. "Best you lay low a while, and possess yourself in patience, as the Good Book says. I can't say more, but you can guess, Bart."

He nodded. "You make sense, son. Miz Lowall will be glad to put me up for a month o' Sundays, did I ask her. Look, there goes the roof. Tod, they didn't leave me stick on stick or stone on stone," he said sadly.

We stayed in the willows until dawn grayed the eastern sky. Then we walked slowly down to the heaps of smoldering ruins that had been the Silver Spring post.

The old man walked ahead, into the center of the square. He turned slowly, to look at each remnant of the shambles. His bent arms came up, the fingers hooked like claws. In every line of his gnarled body hatred was carved. He looked like an Old Testament patriarch calling down the curse of Yahweh on the vicious men who had wrought this destruction. His lips moved without sound.

At last his shoulders slumped and his head drooped. The bitterness of his hate was too much to sustain. My breath caught in my throat. Bart Stoker was a tired, heartbroken old man.

TEN

J OHN STARR WAS at Lazy L when we returned later in the day. I got him aside and gave him my news, all of it. His face grew dark with anger as he listened.

"The devils!" he said. "Well, Tod, that cinches it. We'll wait until they have the horse herd safe in the pens; then we'll clean out the gang, lock, stock, and barrel. I'll work it out with Grant Stevens. We don't want any piecemeal bungling—we want to strike hard, once and for all. You're sure the old man won't go hunting vengeance on his own hook?"

I shook my head. "Not by a damn' sight. You can be sure the old wolf will keep his wits about him. By the way, he knows what I am, but that's all. You're still Stratton."

"Good enough. Tod, you keep on working here; do as Beth Lowall tells you. I'll get word to you in plenty of time when the action begins, or I may see you before then myself."

"What about the Kileys?"

"Play stupid. Too early to turn your hole card. And, Tod—for his presumption about Beth, Rance Kiley is my pigeon."

I gave him a surprised look—at the first-name business, not at the fact that he wanted Kiley. He met my eyes squarely, a faint smile on his face. Without explanation he turned on his heel and strode toward the house.

I was still standing there when, beside me, Sunny spoke. "Are you going to work, bronc fighter, or are you going to stand there all day like a bump on a log?"

I grinned. "No hazer, remember? Ox and Red are still gone."

"I'll haze for you, if you want to work." She came nearer. "Tod, I had to get away from the house. I just can't stand listening to old Bart; I get so furious at the awful thing those men did. I'd—I'd bust something if I stayed."

I put a hand on her shoulder. "All right, kid. Only, I never saw anyone haze horses from a sidesaddle."

For answer she took a few paces in front of me and whirled around. I saw then that the shameless little hussy was wearing a skirt divided in the middle; I hadn't noticed it when she was standing still.

"Who's going to ride sidesaddle?" she asked sweetly.

"Sunny! You get back into the house and put on some decent clothes!" I said, my face hot with embarrassment.

Her face was flushed too, but it was set in defiance.

"You're not ordering me around, Tod Morgan," she said. "My mother made this skirt for me, and I'll wear it if I wish. She says sidesaddles are dangerous. So there!"

"Good God, you women will be wearing p-p-pants next!"

"Tod Morgan, watch your language! I don't intend to wear this outfit in town or to parties. But I guess maybe if the girl riders in Buffalo Bill's Wild West Show can wear clothes like this before thousands of people, I can wear them on our own ranch."

"All right," I said grimly. "But if a girl's going to sit a saddle like a man, she can daggone well saddle her own horse!"

"You think I can't?" she asked, and was gone.

I was sitting on the corral fence, my saddle thrown over the rail, when she rode out of the barn door. She pulled up in front of me, wheeling her mount. She sat there, pink-cheeked and high of head, awaiting my verdict.

It was strange to see a girl riding astride. Still, I had to admit the rigout was modest enough, and practical too. Privately, I had always wondered how they managed to stay on a sidesaddle, even the Goodnight model with the double horn. It must have turned into an unholy instrument of torture by the end of a long ride. Now, in all honesty, I gave my approval.

"Pretty enough," I said. I jumped down from the fence. "You ready to work?"

"I'll haze for you," she said as curtly.

I had to admit that Sunny knew her business, and so did the little mare she rode. I took four of my advanced horses in long runs across the flat, and she held them in line as well as Ox or Red could have done. It was a hot, muggy day, and the sweat was rolling off me as we finished the fourth one. I saw that Sunny's mare was lathered and shiny with sweat. I also noticed that Sunny was standing up in the stirrups whenever she could. A devilish thought came to me.

"I'll take that big gray next," I said. "You still with me?"

"I've never quit a job yet, Tod Morgan," she said.

We took the Roman-nosed gray in the big circle. He was run out and docile when he got back to the corral. I unsaddled, debating whether to school another one. Then I saw that Sunny's mare was bushed, and that the girl was pale beneath her tan. My conscience got the best of me.

"All right, kid, slide down. That's all for the day. I'll take care of the mare for you."

When I came back from the barn, Sunny was still sitting on the bench in the shade. She smiled at me wanly. I felt like a cur.

"Tod," she said, "I'm not sure I can make it to the house."

"The saddle's tougher than you are, eh?"

"I don't think there's any skin left on my—my limbs. A fine hazer I turned out to be."

I helped her up. "You'll be all right, kid. Just rub some goosegrease or bear fat on the—uh—tender spots. You just got too much riding at one time. And I want to say, Sunny, you did a fine job. Good as any man."

"Thanks, Tod. I tried my best. Do you still think I'm a hussy?"

She walked stiffly toward the house, holding to my arm.

"Sure, but a very pretty one," I said, smiling.

Rance Kiley passed us, heading for the barn. His head was down, and he didn't seem to notice us. There, I thought, is a man marked plain for death, though he doesn't know it. I shivered a little at the thought.

In the days that followed, I found myself thinking often of my uncle's attitude toward Beth Lowall. I found hope in it, and a sense of relief. Perhaps the ghost of Mary Reade was at rest at last. If Starr gave his heart to Beth, he would hang up his guns. And the danger trail would end for me as well.

You may think it strange that a young man of twenty, sound of wind and limb, and trained to hold his own in most company, would want to give up the excitement and fame of a life like John Starr's to settle down in the dull routine of ranching. I think I knew then that in that life I was out of my element. Regardless of training and environment, I would always be the Kansas plowboy, more interested in the soil and crops and farm animals than in the wild excitement of gun smoke and fury and sudden death. And, too, into my dreams there kept intruding Sunny's pert face and bright hair.

July came on, hot and dry, with the growling and flicker of distant thunderstorms each evening. I was still working horses with Ox and Red. Of the other three, the Kileys and Bent Lowall, I had seen nothing for days. Bart Stoker, quite chipper again, came and went as he pleased. He seemed to have great plans afoot.

On the night of July 2nd Beth said to me: "Tod, I wish you'd drive Sunny and me to Lewistown tomorrow. We'll take the bay team and the buckboard. We'll have to get an early start."

"Fine with me, ma'am," I said. "I'm getting calluses on top of calluses from sitting those broomtails. Is there a celebration?"

"Is there a celebration?" Ox Pendroy interrupted. "Just about the biggest between the Yellowstone and the Milk. Tod, if it's too fur for you, I'd be glad to drive Miz Lowall."

"Wait a minute. Who was it stayed on Lazy L and worked while two wranglers had themselves a time in Miles about a week ago?"

"Told you it wouldn't work, Ox," Red Beckett said, grinning. "So make up your mind to staying home. Come on, I'll beat you two-three games of crib and you'll feel better."

"*You'll* beat *me?* Why, son, I've made a mint playing crib with punchers like you that couldn't count higher'n fifteen-eight, and half the time fergit His Nobs besides. I'll play you, boy." They headed for the bunkhouse, still arguing.

"Sunny, help Mamie with the dishes," Mrs. Lowall told her daughter. She went out on the stoop with me. "Tod, John Stratton will be in Lewistown," she said. "He says he must see you. Just what is the mysterious secret between you?"

"Nothing disgraceful, Mrs. Lowall. You'll learn in time. But let me say that Stratton is a fine man, and I know he thinks the world and all of you."

"He seems a fine gracious gentleman," she said, with the faintest of blushes.

I leaned a hip on the log railing, finding the porch pleasantly cool behind the screen of wild cucumber vines. I watched her pace back and forth.

"Everything is at sixes and sevens, Tod," she said, sighing. "So many things could happen. I'm terribly worried."

"About your boy?"

"Yes. He's so utterly under the sway of the Kileys that sometimes he seems like an utter stranger to me. For the moment, thank heaven, he's safe in Miles City, while Shan and Rance are at Burnt Rock. I've even sent Bart Stoker on a trumped-up errand to Miles to keep an eye on Benton."

"That should help. There isn't anything wrong with Bent— yet. But, Mrs. Lowall, a cleanup is coming. When it starts, get your boy under cover and keep him there."

"Oh, I'll try. But I must say it: Bent is as wild and as careless as his father was before him. I think sometimes that I have failed as a mother. I may yet be able to keep him from turning the wrong way. I love my son, Tod, even while I see his faults. And I'd fight you or John Stratton or anyone else who threatened Benton. Fight like a tigress."

"You've got spirit, ma'am," I said admiringly. "Let's hope it doesn't come to that. But the longer Bart keeps him away from this part of the country, the better."

"Is it coming that soon?"

"That's not for me to say. I'm just a small cog in the machine. But I'd say the signs were right."

She came up to me, put her hands on my shoulders, and looked into my face with pleading in her fine eyes.

"Tod, help Benton. For my sake, protect him."

Pitying her, unable to resist the sincerity of her request, I gave her a slow nod. "I'll do my damnedest, Mrs. Lowall." I told her.

ELEVEN

HAVE NOTED, then and later, that in the middle of a time of action and excitement there can come an odd period of calm, like the eye of a hurricane, perhaps. The long trip to Lewis-town had that unreal, dreamy quality about it. Afterward I found myself remembering it when many details of the wild days that followed had dimmed into a haze of gun smoke and a welter of confused sound. Yet in that peaceful interlude there was a sense of foreboding, as if the tension that was building up around Lazy L was stretching itself to the limits of endurance. Something must give, and soon.

The light dew was still on the long grass when we started. Open wildflowers starred the meadows. The team of broncs was about two-thirds harness broke, and they wanted to run. I let them, with Sunny and her mother hanging on for dear life until the horses had run off the first edge of their eagerness.

By noon we were at McDonald Creek. South of us were the white crowns of the Snowies. Against the horizon to the north-west lay the ridges of the Judiths. The little creek was clear and bright, the grass long and lush. And the picnic basket held, roughly, enough for the complement at Fort Maginnis. So it was a fine nooning we had, and a fine meal.

The women wandered off. I dozed in the shade of the wagon, but aware, nevertheless, of the bright sun and the clacking of the grasshoppers and the cropping of the horses nearby. I came up standing, my six-gun in my hand, when a shriek came sharp across the meadow.

False alarm. For laughter followed the scream. I walked toward the screening willow, whistling to herald my presence. Beth Lowall came up from the creek bed, reaching for my hand to assist her. She was laughing hard, and it struck me that she was purely beautiful. What a partner for John Starr!

"Sunny went wading in the creek," she explained, bursting with laughter. "She stepped into a hole and went *way* in. And that water is pure ice. Talk about a wet hen!"

"Let's go back to the rig, then," I said, taking her arm. "She won't stay damp long in this weather. Mrs. Lowall, that girl of yours is the dangdest one for getting into things."

Beth looked up at me, almost slyly.

"But notice, Tod, that she also gets herself out of them again."

"She could charm a bird out of a bush," I admitted.

"She's an imp to Satan. If only her brother had something of her quality. Instead, he has a genius for doing the wrong thing at the wrong time."

"A few more years will change that," I said, as if I meant it.

"I wish I could believe that. No. Tod, he's like his father. Tall Tom borrowed a horse once. Before the chain that started was broken by his death, he was mixed up with thieves, rustlers, and horse stealers. Not that Tom didn't prefer the company of such."

"Men are funny critters," I said, meaning it. I don't know why she threw her head back laughing fit to kill.

As I backed the team into the traces, Sunny came running across the meadow, her golden hair flying, her white feet twinkling under the damp-dark hem of her dress. She was carrying her shoes and stockings.

"A fine day for a swim," I said.

"Very refreshing," she said, her nose in the air. Before she knew what was happening, I picked her up and half-tossed her into the buckboard. I was about to climb up to the seat when I spotted the lemonade jug still sitting on the shadow of a willow. I retrieved it and set it in the back of the buckboard. Then

I unwound the reins from the whipstock, shook them out, and clucked to the horses.

"Some people are sure forgetful," I said.

"Aren't they just?" Sunny said. "Tod, it's lucky you remembered that jug. We might want a cool drink later."

I just about exploded, for it was Sunny who had left the jug, and she knew it. Just in time, I saw that she was angling to get me riled, so I kept my mouth shut, though it wasn't easy. Daggone women, I thought. They always manage somehow to crowd a man into a tight and leave him there.

We came to the end of our long road in the fading twilight. Ahead, the lamps of Lewistown twinkled. All along Spring Creek the campfires of the metis glowed orange and umber among their carts. We splashed through the creek and turned northwest. The business street was crowded with men and rigs and saddle horses. Beyond, in the quiet of a back street, Mrs. Lowall directed me to a large frame house glowing in the dusk with new white paint. I helped the women down and worked the luggage loose.

The door of the house flew open and a buxom blond girl came running down the shaft of yellow light. She enfolded Sunny in a great hug. There followed such squealing and crying and talking as I never heard. Like barnyard geese, seemed to me.

"Come on, Tod," Mrs. Lowall said, laughing. I picked up the valises and followed her to the house.

The Johnsons' house was the grandest I was ever in. Lars Johnson owned the Mercantile, so he could afford it. He was a stout man of forty-five, with a handclasp that would have splintered a pine board.

"Come right in, young Morgan. Ve got a houseful; yust a few minutes ago the Busbys come in from Horse Heaven country. By golly, ve have a lot of fun. My vife and daughter, they fix plenty good Scandinavian food. You like a small nip schnapps, Tod?"

I shook my head. I was looking around the house. My, but it was fine and bright and new; everything was of the best.

"Nice, eh?" Lars Johnson asked, pleased at my interest. "The boards, dey were the first cut on my new little sawmill up in the Judiths. Glass windows come from St. Louis. Curtains, carpets, all the best. No house like this even in Maiden, Tod. Come now, you got your carpetbag? Ve squeeze you in somewhere."

"No, don't bother, Mr. Johnson," I said. "I'll find a place over at the hotel."

He guffawed and clouted me on the shoulder. "You t'ink so? Vy, dey sleeping t'ree in a bed now, among the mouses and the bedboogs. No, son, maybe house is overflowin' vit vimmen, but ve sleep you somewhere. By golly, how you t'ink you like the loft in my new barn? Full of fresh hay, it make a nice soft bed?"

"That's my meat," I said. I had been dreading the prospect of coping with all those women. Leading the way with a lantern, Johnson showed me to the barn, with its ample hayloft and highpiled prairie hay. A canvas tarp and a couple blankets, and I was set.

At the foot of the ladder, Johnson said, "Vait a minute, Tod." He disappeared into the tack room, then came back with a bottle.

"You sure you don't want small drink schnapps before supper? Then I have one."

And he took a good one, his Adam's apple bobbing like a piston in his throat. He sighed with solid satisfaction, pushed the cork back in the bottle, then hid the bottle again.

"Now ve eat," he said, grinning.

Mrs. Johnson, a bustling, red-faced woman, was a jim-dandy cook. But what with her and Mrs. Lowall and Sunny and Emmy and Mrs. Busby and her two daughters, Johnson and Busby and I didn't have much of a show. There was so much woman talk and squealing and giggling among the girls that I could hardly get down my second piece of pie.

We escaped to the parlor. But Busby was one of those backward little men who converse mostly in throat clearings and grunts. And after sneaking a couple of more doses of schnapps

Lars Johnson grew red-faced and sleepy. So I begged off, and with a lighted lantern found my way to the barn and to bed. It was blessedly quiet except for the occasional stamp of a horse's hoof or the rub of hide against a stall. I was asleep between two thoughts.

I came awake in gray dawnlight, and without doubt it was the Fourth. Already I could hear the snap of Chinese crackers and the occasional boom of a fired anvil. The roosters were making their morning brag. Nearby a cow groaned because of the heavy state of her udder, begging somebody to do something about it. I lay still in my hay bed for a while, warm and lazy and comfortable. But something of the excitement of the day got into me, and I piled out, shivering in the cool morning air.

After breakfast, as the sun climbed higher, the day grew noisier. Even though the small boys had shot off all their firecrackers by noon, the men took up the din with their pistols, as their mood became lubricated. Now and then some especially hardy soul would unlimber a shotgun and blast away.

We all went down to the parade. I was amazed at the number of people who had gathered in the little town. They must literally have come from hundreds of miles around. The ladies watched the parade from the safety of the surrey, but Johnson, Busby, and I mingled with the throng. The two of them would slip into Crowley's saloon now and then for a quick one. I remained outside to look out for the safety of the windows on the Mercantile, as Johnson had asked me to do.

The parade was like ten thousand others that day in ten thousand towns across America: the bearded man leading it, the G.A.R., Confederate Veterans, the Knights Templars, and the Grace Sunday school, each child waving a cheesecloth flag. Around and beside and behind them were all the small boys in town and every dog. Lifting it along, an improvised band, with an overabundance of flutes but with a dandy drummer, brought up the rear, only slightly out of tune and time.

When it broke up near the end of Main Street, we gathered to hear the classic Fourth of July address. Today it was given in a rich brogue by an Irish politician from Butte City, not long from the Old Sod himself. He must have been thirsty, for he finished his remarks in forty-five minutes. But the crowd didn't mind.

I had no mind for a coachman's chore, but before I knew it Busby and Johnson had ducked into Crowleys' again, so I had to drive the ladies back to the Johnson house in the surrey. Through lunch, the four young ladies had a glorious time ragging me. I'll bet my face was red as a lobster during the whole meal. I sure couldn't handle them. But, deep down, I kind of enjoyed it, even when they made me feel like a fool.

The two men didn't come back, so it was up to me to squire the girls to the races, on the flat above town. Before I could get them all in the surrey, there was a great gathering of gloves and parasols and handkerchiefs, with much chatter and bustle. At last they were ready. We drove off with Sunny sitting beside me. In spite of the hot day, she looked as if she had just stepped from a bandbox. She was as pretty as a picture, and my heart gave a funny little flutter when I looked at her. Nor did I stop looking.

At the improvised, dusty track, I let the girls out, then found a place to tie up the team. Before I joined them, the Busby girls were already in the company of a couple young cowpokes, and shortly afterward left with them. The meeting must have been planned. I wondered if I should protest, but Sunny and Emmy seemed unperturbed, so I guessed it was all right. I spread a blanket on a grassy place with a good view of the finish line, and we sat down. The girls raised their parasols against the blazing July sun.

Shortly after the third race Uncle Sam joined us. He was still wearing the striped pants and star-studded vest he had worn leading the parade. I saw now that his red, white, and blue top hat was made of cardboard.

"Sunny and Tod, I'd like for to have you meet Mister Bob James." Emmy said with a blush.

"Won't you join us, Bob?" I asked, shaking hands.

"Don't mind if I do," he said. He folded his long legs and sank down next to Emmy. Taking off the stovepipe hat, he fanned himself with it, remarking about the heat.

"Yes, you're melting," Emmy said. With a quick grab, she snatched off his crepe beard. We laughed as he yelped in sudden pain.

The races were no great shakes for speed, but most of them were close and exciting. A surprising amount of money was changing hands on each race. But Bob James and I didn't bet. The presence of the two girls was enough stimulation.

In a lull between races, James said: "Say, Morgan, did you hear what happened last night? They caught Sam McKenzie red-handed with a couple of stolen horses two miles below the fort. They hung him."

"Sudden justice, eh?" I asked. "Who pulled the rope?"

"Reece Anderson and some of his punchers. McKenzie was one of the slickest horse thieves in these parts. A man's horses might be safe with the 'breed gone."

"Was he the only thief around here?" Sunny asked with a touch of scorn.

James grinned ruefully. "No, you're right, Miss Lowall. There's plenty more as bad or worse. For instance, what do you think of them two?" He flicked a thumb at two men who were making their way slowly through the crowd.

Down the long road with John Starr, I had learned to read the signs. This pair made the hackles rise on the back of my neck. They were pure trouble. Everything about them marked the true desperado. They were dressed in worn and greasy buckskins, a costume almost never seen any more. One of them was lean and gray and hard chiseled of face. The other was like something disclosed by a turned stone, the eyes shifty, the mouth cruel. He wore his hair gathered like a woman's, a twist of filthy string around the long horsetail of it. Each carried two pistols and a bowie knife. They looked as bitter and mean as old timberwolves.

"Two to fight shy of," I said to James.

"They've been making big brag around town," James told me. "The hairy one's Charley Fallon; the tall one's called Rattlesnake Jake Owen. By their say-so, anyhow. New around here."

"They're hitting the booze. Let's keep an eye on them."

At the last race, with the sun beginning to slant down the afternoon sky, Fallon and Owen placed bets for the first time. They must have bet heavily. The race was a good one, but the bay pony came in a half-length ahead of the black they had chosen.

They were bad losers. They stomped around, elbowing roughly through the crowd. They came toward us, finishing their bottle of whisky. Fallon smashed the empty bottle on a rock.

"C'mon, Jake, let's clean out this town," he said loudly.

But Owen had caught sight of Bob James' Uncle Sam costume. For some reason it infuriated Owen. He came over to us. Without warning, he jerked out a pistol and smashed James over the head with it. The blow dazed James and he sprawled forward. Owen stood over him, the cocked pistol aimed at James' head.

"Crawl in the dust, damn you!" he growled. "Crawl like a snake, if you want to keep on livin'."

I was on my knees, my hand streaking for my gun. But Emmy Johnson was crowding against me, her hand tight on my wrist.

"No, Tod, no!" she breathed in terror. "He'll kill Bob! Wait for a better chance."

Even in his dazed condition, Bob James thought fast. Under Owen's gun, he did exactly what I would have done—he crawled, inching along in the dust like a grotesque snake. Owen, snarling, watched him get farther and farther away. Then a sudden change of mood came on him. He forgot Bob James.

"Morgan, give me that gun!" James said, his voice shaking with humiliation and anger. "I'm going after that man and kill him."

"You'll do no such thing!" Emmy said, brushing dust from his clothes. "Tod wanted to do it, but I wouldn't let him."

"The man richly deserved it," Sunny said. "But, Tod, I'm glad you didn't. Those men are vicious brutes. Any number of innocent people might have been hurt. Remember, you're a bronc snapper, not a gun fighter."

"Maybe you're right," I said, folding up the blanket. I led the way toward the rig, a little ashamed of myself though there was some merit to Sunny's reasoning.

"See you all at the dance tonight," Bob James said, tipping his hat. He strode off, still smarting with his humiliation before his girl. Nor did I blame him.

I had just helped the girls down to the wooden sidewalk in front of the Johnson home when Lars Johnson came rushing out. He barely nodded to the girls.

"Tod, yoost in time! Drive me down to the store. A boy come running with the message; there's bad trouble. Two men going to shoot up the place. Oh, my big plate windows!"

I jumped into the seat, then the rig sank to one side under Johnson's ponderous weight. I flicked the reins of the cayuses, and they took off on a dead run. Johnson leaned forward, hanging onto his hat, his face red with schnapps and anger.

He pointed, and I turned the rig into an alley, raising the inside wheels off the ground. I braced myself against the dash and brought them up all standing at the platform in back of Johnson's Mercantile. We piled out of the rig and into the back door of the store.

TWELVE

LABS JOHNSON UNLOCKED the front door of the store and flung it open. By ones and twos men hurried in, breathing fast, shock and anger plain on their faces. The sound of firing in the street was heavier now. Johnson asked no questions. He unlocked two tall cupboards and flung rifles from them onto the counter. I broke open a case of cartridges and began handing them out by the handful.

"Never seen anything like it," one of the men said, thumbing shells into the loading gate of the rifle. "Yellin' that they'll clean out the town, firing at anything that moves. The dam' fools don't seem to care if they git killed or not."

"Berserker!" Lars Johnson muttered. He nodded his head.

From outside came yells, then the snap of a small-caliber pistol. A man charged in the door, bent low. Behind him a rifle boomed. Glass smashed tinkling to the floor of the room. The men inside ducked and so did I. Lars Johnson groaned and put his palms to his ears. There was brief firing. Powder smoke drifted across the room.

"You all right, Doane?" someone yelled at the newcomer.

"By the skin of my teeth. That crazy Owen was cutting down on me when I put a .22 into his hand. Didn't seem to faze him. So I left the scene—pronto."

"You might as well bite a man, Joe, as even gutshoot him with that peashooter," a man jeered.

"Give him a bellyache about next week, though," Doane said, grinning.

The firing had slackened. I went to the broken window. I could see Owen near the end of the street, where an itinerant photographer had set up his tent. He lurched a little, and his stained buckskins were stained worse than ever, but he was still alert, and looked deadly.

Now came Fallon riding hard down the street. Rifles and pistols blazed furiously. A shot must have hit the man, for he swayed in the saddle. He reached the other end of the street. Somehow his pistol belt came undone and dropped to the ground. Calm as Judas, he stopped his horse. Leaning far over, he picked up the belt. He glanced back and saw that Owen had not followed him.

I saw Charley Fallon do something then which I consider the bravest thing I ever saw in my life. He wheeled his horse. With complete disregard of the guns blazing at him from close range, he rode the full length of the street. I'll never know how he made it. But there he was, jumping off his horse, pulling his rifle from the saddle boot and standing beside Owen in front of the photographer's tent. And the two of them shooting at anything that moved along the street.

The ordinary cowboy, wrangler, or ranch hand was never any great shakes as a marksman. As a specialist, I knew that. I shook my head at the storm of lead that whizzed ineffectively along the street, knowing it was as dangerous to the citizens as it was to the two desperadoes standing so calmly in the street, firing methodically, keeping their assailants back under cover.

A green hand with a gun, a man full of Independence Day enthusiasm and Crowley's forty-rod, was a dangerous character when he started spraying lead around the countryside. There had to be an end to this. I stepped forward, about to take a Winchester away from one of the whooping townsmen and use it properly.

Down the street, two men broke from cover, dashing across for some imagined better vantage point. Fallon dropped to one knee. He fired three shots as fast as he could work the lever of the rifle.

One man's hat jumped and flew off. The man dived, rolling into the dust of the street, and lay still. The second man threw up his arms. His knees sagged as if disjointed. He crumpled face down into the dirt and lay there with the flaccid finality of sudden death.

"My God, they've kilt Ben Smith!" a man at the window yelled. "And Joe Jackson's down. Looks like he's been hurted."

I saw the first man's hand scrabble in the dirt, saw him flex one knee under him. At the movement Owen pegged a shot at him. A gout of dirt plumed beside Jackson's boot, and the slug whined off down the street.

I didn't need to think. Before Owen could fire again I was out of the door and running toward the downed man. A bullet cracked past my ear as I stooped over him. I had a glimpse of his face; then I swung him to my shoulder and was running to safety. In moments I was back in the store, dumping the inert form on the counter. I stepped back, mopping my sweaty face.

Then I gaped in surprise as Jackson sat up, grinning at us. He wiped a hand across the seeping bullet graze on his cheek, looked at the red ooze of it. He felt his head, pulling at the hair. He looked at me.

"Thanks, kid," he said. "Damn' hyena shot off a lock of me golden tresses. That's too close for comfort."

"Well, damn you!" I said. "You were playing possum."

"Doin' a good job of it, too," he said. "Longhair thought he'd kilt me. No need for you to come a-runnin'."

"You'd moved that knee one more time, you'd be stone dead," I said grimly. "Fools who can't stay under cover ..."

"What's going on here?" John Starr asked from behind me.

I turned. "I just dragged this buzzard out of the line of fire, Mr. Stratton. He nearly got himself killed."

He looked at me with an air of disgust. "The hard way, wasn't it? If you had killed those crazy renegades, you could have walked out to save this man." With the flashing speed that was typical of him, he plucked a Winchester from the nearest man. He checked the magazine, hefted the gun, and rubbed a thumb across the bead of the front sight. In three steps he was out on the sidewalk, facing the two men without cover of any kind.

I shook my head. I knew with a sense of shame that Starr was right. But in the back of my mind was a reluctance to bring even these two brutes to their deaths by my own hand. I had been hoping, I knew then, that the storm of lead would take its toll without my assistance. There went the Kansas plowboy again.

As cool and unconcerned as if he were at a turkey shoot, John Starr brought the rifle to his shoulder. He fired, levered in another shell, fired again. He lowered the gun with an air of finality.

In front of the photographer's tent, Owen took a twisting fall into the dirt and was still. Fallon dropped his rifle. Slowly he crumpled to his knees. He struggled to draw a pistol, managed to fire it once into the ground just in front of him, and then pitched forward, dead.

John Starr stepped back into the store. He laid the rifle on the counter. "If you can't use the tools, don't try the trade," he said to the other men. He and I stood back as they surged toward the door, anxious to get a look at the dead men. In seconds we two were alone in the emptied store.

"Tod, you're a damned fool," he said. But he never again spoke of my foolhardy act. "You hear about McKenzie? Tod, there's blood on the moon. Get the women back to the ranch as soon as you can. We're winding this thing up as fast as they get that stolen horse herd here."

"What do you want me to do?"

"Stick close to Lazy L. You'll hear from me in a day or so. In the meantime I want someone to look out for Mrs. Lowall. No telling what the Kileys will do. It worries me. I—well, I think a great deal of Beth Lowall."

I tried to read his face. But he was smoothing his mustache with his characteristic gesture, and his hand hid his lips. His eyes said nothing.

"All right," I answered. "If I can make them leave."

"I'll stop long enough to talk to Beth. They'll be ready."

"One thing, Uncle John," I said in a low tone. "When the cleanup comes—well, she loves that whelp of hers. And the way I see it, he's going to be right spang in the middle of trouble. What if we have to ..."

"It's up to us to keep him in the clear," Starr said, frowning. "Right now he's in Miles with Bart Stoker keeping an eye on him. Maybe he'll stay there."

"Fat chance. And old Bart knows I'm a range detective. I had to tell him on the night of the raid on Silver Spring."

"That's all right. He's been on Grant Stevens' payroll a long time. Besides, he hates the outlaws more than ever since the raid. I wish he'd forget his one-man feud. I'm worried about the old hellion."

"Just so he rides herd on Benton Lowall. But what if the roundup corrals the kid with it? What then?"

He looked at me grimly. "Tod, we'll have to cross that bridge when we come to it. But promise me one thing—for the sake of Beth and Sunny Lowall, do everything you can to keep the young pup out of trouble. I don't want to have to plead his case to Grant Stevens and Stuart and Fergus. But I'd even do that, for Beth's sake."

"That doesn't sound like you."

"Perhaps I've grown tired of the long trail," he said wearily. "Perhaps old ghosts want at last to be left to the peace of the grave."

It was the first time I had ever seen my uncle uncertain of himself. It touched me deeply.

"I promise, Uncle John, that I'll keep an eye on Bent Lowall," I said. "Though afterward I'll beat the whelp within an inch of his life—I'll promise *him* that. And I'll stand between the Lowall women and trouble, no matter what. I've—I've got a stake of my own there. At least I hope so."

"Good boy, Tod," John Starr said, clapping me on the shoulder. "Now, I'll vamos and talk to Beth. To make things look natural, you stroll over there and take a look at the bodies. People would think it strange if you didn't. Then get moving for the ranch."

I would sooner have taken a beating, but, as he said, we had to play our roles through the last act. I pushed my way into the crowd, looked briefly at the torn carcasses, and stepped back.

The inevitable know-it-all was expounding loudly. "Yes, sir, nine bullets in Rattlesnake, eleven in Owen. I counted 'em. Any one of 'em fatal—in time, that is. And I kin show you the two I put in 'em myself."

"Took the horse buyer to put 'em down for keeps, though, Bubber," someone jeered.

"Lucky shots, lucky shots," Bubber said quickly. "Now stand aside, ever'body. The photographer's gonna take their pitchers."

"You hear who they was, Bubber?" a man asked.

"Sure, had a telegraft a while ago. From Wyomin'. They was killers, horse thieves, and gen'ral badmen. Wanted in Buffalo, wanted in Grand Junction, wanted in the Nation. Me and the rest of you boys done a dam' good day's work, I tell you."

"You'll get a leather medal for sure, Bubber," someone yelled. The crowd guffawed. I left.

Passing the store, I saw Lars Johnson sadly studying the shambles the fight had made of it. He picked up a dropped rifle, looked at it sadly, and put it gently on the counter.

"I'm going to take Mrs. Lowall and Sunny back to Lazy L tonight, Mr. Johnson," I told him.

"I von't say no, Tod. Best they are away from trouble. There is more to come. That I know, for sure."

"We are agreed on that. Looks like the whole country might go up like a powder keg."

"I don't like it. But what can a man do? This thing today …" He gestured at the shambles around him. "Tod, vat makes men like that? Animals, yet. They kill and kill, den somebody kills dem. So much good and trugh and beauty in dis old world. Yet men spoil it with cruelty and hate and killing. You tell me, Tod?"

I had seen so much more of it, more brutal, more senseless, than he had, despite my fewer years. But I was no nearer the answer than Lars Johnson.

"It's beyond me," I told him, and I was sincere. "When I figure it out, if I do, I'll tell you. So long."

When I got to the Johnson house, the women were packed and ready. I hitched up and brought the team around. I expected feminine tears, but I began then to understand what I know now—that when the chips are down women cast off the trappings of sentiment, and exhibit a cold hard practicality that few men can equal.

The moon had set, and only the glow of the hard bright stars was lighting our way when we finally rattled across the ford and into the yard at Lazy L. Sunny was asleep, a dead weight against my shoulder. I helped her down, and Mrs. Lowall and I walked her across the yard and into the house, but I don't think she even woke up then. Mrs. Lowall put her hand on mine.

I grinned at her in the lamplight and went to put the team away.

It was the fifth of July, 1884.

The Kileys came riding in the next morning, riding in from nowhere. Shan came down to the corral, where Sunny was watching me gentle a pretty buckskin horse for her. The minute I saw Shan, I knew he was on the prod. He leaned his forearms along the rail.

They tell me you were the big hero in Lewistown yesterday," he said.

"Too much lead flying for me. I hunted cover with the rest of them."

"Huh! Running out into the street to drag in that fool Joe Jackson. Lot of nerve that took, a whole town against two lone men!"

"They asked for it," I said. I flipped off the headstall and turned the buckskin loose with a light slap on the flank. I walked toward Kiley. "How come you know so much about it?"

"Not much goes on around here without me knowing," he said darkly. "I come to get Bent. Where is he?"

"Billings, Miles City, Fort Benton. Who knows? You're his pal, aren't you?" Sunny asked.

"You see him, you tell him to get over to Burnt Rock, pronto. That is, if he expects to earn a share."

"A share of what?" she asked.

"None of your business. Just tell him."

"Some more devilment, I suppose. My brother would have been better off if he had never seen you, Shan Kiley," she said spiritedly.

I pulled off my riding gloves and tucked them into my belt. I walked over to the fence post and took down my gun belt and holster. I buckled the belt around my middle and settled the gun low on my right thigh. I saw Rance Kiley coming down from the house, his face suffused with anger.

I walked over toward Sunny, letting her continue her verbal sparring with Shan. Out of the corner of my eye I watched Rance approach. I ducked through the bars of the corral, coming up on Shan from the outside. Listening, I grinned a little, for the girl had Shan buffaloed.

"I'll thank you to leave my brother alone," she was saying. "You're a troublemaker, a lazy no-good and, I don't doubt, a plain thief. And your father's no better."

"Don't forget, Miss Biggety, we own part of Lazy L," Shan said. "One of these days—"

"One of these days we'll throw the Lowalls clean off'n it," Rance Kiley said, coming up. "We don't have to put up with no insults like Beth Lowall jest give me."

I stepped forward. "How could Mrs. Lowall insult you, Kiley? I think it's impossible to insult a blackleg like you—a thief, a robber, a man who hires killers for his dirty work."

"What do you mean?" His face was ominous.

"I've got friends on the owlhoot trail. The word is around how you had your killers stage a fake fight in that Billings saloon. Faked it so Tom Lowall was lying dead in the sawdust when it was over.

"Tall Tom was a friend of mine. Why should I do a thing like that?"

"For an interest in Lazy L. For the stupid idea of ridding Mrs. Lowall of a husband, so you could court her and win the rest of Lazy L. Kiley, you ought to know that a renegade like you wouldn't stand a chance on God's green earth of winning a fine woman like Beth Lowall."

"Listen, you fool horse wrangler, I've got a mind to—"

"It's all right with me. Go ahead and draw," I said pleasantly.

To my surprise he did. Perhaps I had goaded him too far; perhaps he had forgotten how badly I had shaded him the other time; or maybe it was the presence of his son. At any rate he came up with iron in his fist.

I thought fast. Without a leader the bandit gangs might go under cover for a while, and the whole plan of the cleanup would be lost. I contented myself with shooting the gun out of his hand. He yelled at the shock and the pain of cut fingers and numbed nerves. I swung a glance at Shan. He was holding his hands ostentatiously away from his body, chest high.

"All right," I said. "You two are through on Lazy L. You have fifteen minutes to pack your warbags and get gone. Neither of you has now, or has ever had, any legal claim to any part of Lazy L, even if you did kill Tom Lowall to get it. So from now on, if you set a foot on Lazy L ground you're dead men. You want to argue?"

Shan Kiley licked his lips, opened his mouth, and closed it again without saying a word. He swiveled his head to look at his father. Rance was holding the numb wrist of his right hand tight with his left. He was staring at me with a look of such pure hatred that if I hadn't dealt with other men like him, it would have given me bad dreams. I stared back at him, my face as granite hard as I could make it. His glance wavered first.

The two of them made the deadline with two minutes to spare. I stood watching them, the two men and three horses, until they were across the creek and heading up the hill. Then I turned to Sunny.

"We'd better go up to the house and tell your mother about the Kileys," I said.

"Was all that you said true, Tod?" she asked breathlessly.

"As Gospel," I told her.

THIRTEEN

ETH LOWELL HEARD US out. Sunny told her of our run-in with the Kileys, and I went on to tell the story of Tom Lowall's death. When we had finished, Beth walked over to the window, drew aside the curtains, and stared out across the yard. She stood there until the silence became almost too much to bear. At last she turned to face us, her shoulders straight and her head held high.

"It is out now," she said, with something of relief in her voice. "Sunny, listen to me. And you, Tod. For after today I will never say this again. I want it buried with the dead past." She drew a long breath, touching slim fingers to the table top as if to support herself.

"Sunny, your father, Benton's father, was a weak man. He had charm and wild courage. And I—I loved him. Even at the last, when he had given me every reason to hate him, there was still some love in my heart. But there was something lacking in Tom. He was mercurial, easily bored. You could almost call him shiftless. He wanted the easy life, the exciting life, stimulation and change and new experiences. Tom never quite grew up. As far as Lazy L was concerned, after the first year he was more of a burden than a help. In the years since you were born, Sunny, your father had never turned his hand for a day's work on this ranch. But you know that. You were here as a growing girl."

She stopped, gathering her strength. "What you don't know, my dear, is that your father at least three times almost destroyed or lost Lazy L—by gambling or reckless borrowing or by illegal acts. Each time I managed to save it. But each time my love for Tom withered a little more. I learned to close my eyes to his affairs, the 'breed girl he kept one winter in Maiden, the dance-hall girl he visited in Fort Benton. But when he jeopardized the ranch that was yours and Benton's, I came near to hating him. I didn't wish him dead—the world even now is an emptier place without his reckless charm. But life is easier without him, for a woman with two children to raise and a living to make."

"Is that why you didn't challenge Kiley's claim to a part of the ranch?" I asked.

She nodded. "It was easier to let him stay, paying him a share, than to bring it to a head, and perhaps lose the whole thing. And Kiley did work to build up the place, until the last year or so. Which is more than my husband ever did."

"Well, don't worry about him. I think Mr. Kiley is gone—for good."

"I hope so. If we can get protection from the outlaws with-out Rance Kiley, I can run Lazy L with the help of Sunny and Benton."

"Benton?" I asked, with some irony.

There was sadness in her eyes. "Tod, my son is weak, even as his father was, but without his father's charm. I know that. But away from evil influences, I think he'll settle down. I pray on my knees every night that he will. For I'm his mother, Tod. He is my firstborn. Everything a mother's tears and a mother's love can do for him, I will do. And more. I'll never give up."

"If my mother had lived, I think she would have felt the same," I assured her. Though I said it doubting that Benton would ever come up to her hopes. And I think that she feared the same thing. "But, Mrs. Lowall," I went on, "I judge that you have some hint of what is about to happen in the range-land. For God's sake, promise me—and you too, Sunny—that you will say nothing to anyone. And that includes Bent. A single word in the wrong ear might mean death to me and to many other men. This is war, Mrs. Lowall. We hope it will soon be over, with as little bloodshed as possible. But I want your promise."

"You have it, Tod," she told me.

"I swear it, Tod," Sunny said, her eyes wide.

"Thank God Bent is safe in Miles," Mrs. Lowall went on. She put an arm about her daughter's shoulders and hugged her tightly. "If he had half the spirit and ability of this one, I wouldn't worry about him so much." She gave her daughter a half-turn and a light pat. "Start preparing supper, dear. Mamie went to Miles and won't be back for a few days. You're the cook."

Sunny made a little face, and I winked at her as she went through the door to the kitchen.

"Tod, I'm also worried about something else," Mrs. Lowall said, going to the door with me. "Is John Stratton mixed up in this too?"

I turned my hat in my hands, studying how to answer her. "He hasn't said anything to you?" I asked.

"No."

"Then I can't say anything. It's up to him."

She stepped back two paces, then made a sweeping gesture with her open hands. "Tod, look at me. I'm not an old woman. After Tom and I grew apart, when he began flaunting his affairs in my face, night after night I would lie sleepless in the long darkness. And I would pray: 'Lord, have pity. Send me a true man. A man who will love me and cherish me and respect me.' I'm shameless, Tod. With Tom gone, I still pray that prayer. And I think the Lord answered me when he sent John Stratton here."

Her eyes were shining, her pride and love and happiness showing clear in her beautiful face. Yet Beth's words brought me a certain dismay.

"He's told you nothing?" I asked. "Of his past, his name, his work?"

Her chin went up proudly. "Nor does he need to. Tod, I know John Stratton. He is a good man. He's honest and fine and

true. No matter what he is or does, I'm deeply in love with him."
Then, with the color high in her cheeks, she said, "But if you ever
breathe a single word of this to John—"

"Your secret is safe with me, Mrs. Lowall," I said. "And … I'm
glad."

"Thank you, Tod," she said, and turned away.

Going to the bunkhouse, I met Ox and Red coming from the
corral. I gave them the story of my tangle with the Kileys.

Ox Pendroy whistled softly. "Good for you, Tod. 'Bout time
them two got their needin's. You sure got a nerve, though. Them
boys are plenty salty."

"Not in my book," I said. "You think they have any tieup with
the rustlers?" It was a blunt question. But it was time to find out
where they stood.

"O' course they have," Red Beckett said positively. "The
Kileys been wavin' big money around for the last year. At the
same time they've been mighty friendly with Jumbo Eiler and
Art Cobb and the rest of the gang that hangs out at Ingersoll's.
Wouldn't surprise me if more than one Lazy L bronc didn't go
down the long trail to the Nations or up to Fort Calgary."

"Yeah," Ox put in, "but a man dassen't hint at it, even to Miz
Lowall. Too many men found dead in a alder thicket around
here, jest because they talked out of turn."

"Then why do you talk now?" I asked sharply.

Ox looked startled. "I dunno, Tod. Only, seems to me,
after Sam McKenzie, and them two at Lewistown, that the
country's gettin' up on its hind legs and kickin'. I got a big fat
hunch that the day of reckonin' is at hand, as the Good Book
says."

"I can give you this much, Ox: your hunch is right," I told
him. "Where do you boys stand? Will you ride and shoot, and
tail onto the end of a rope over a cottonwood branch?"

Beckett frowned. "Tod, we didn't hire out as no gun-
slicks. Ox and me ain't fightin' men. But we're sick and tired of

kowtowin' to hardcases like Jumbo Eiler and Rance Kiley. And tired of seein' an honest, hard-workin' widow like Miz Lowall put upon."

We turned at the drumming of hoofs. A 'breed kid on a paintpot pinto was racing into the yard. He pulled the horse up all standing and handed me a sealed envelope.

"Me from Woods' Point. Meestair Marsh say find Tod Morgan, give him paper, him give you one dollair," the kid said. He was dressed in breechclout and leggings. The toes of his moccasins were scuffed through. His bare upper body streamed with sweat, the ribcage going in and out with his breathing, so thinly fleshed that every rib stood out.

I flipped him a silver cartwheel. He caught it deftly, bit it with fine white teeth, and slipped it into his belt pouch. He drummed on the pinto's taut hide with his heels and wheeled away in a cloud of dust.

I opened the envelope. It was a telegram from Fort Maginnis to Woods' Point:

"Ore will be delivered at smelter approximately seventh. Come early for a good time, bring friends. Counting on you for quick delivery and collection of all accounts. Be sure to cancel Fort Benton trip.

"It's come, boys," I said to Ox and Red.

"War is declared, you mean?"

"For sure. Stratton says the big stolen herd will be delivered at Burnt Rock day after tomorrow. He hopes to hit the, whole bunch of rustlers at one swoop. Will you ride with me at moonrise tomorrow night?"

"Ride all night and fight in the mornin'," Ox said. "Well, one thing's a cinch—them nippers won't be awake when we hit 'em. They're too all-fired lazy."

All the next day I was subdued. There would be fighting and death at the end of the night. Sometimes I felt a lift of excitement, but mainly a serious worry. Not so much physical fear as a dull doubt whether violence solved anything. I knew that I would do what I had to do, and that the violence which would destroy the gangs was but an echo of the violence they themselves had wrought. But it seemed to me there must be a better way to solve such things. I guess I was growing up.

Somehow the long day dragged to its weary end. At supper everyone was quiet, with thoughts turned inward. I had told Mrs. Lowall earlier in the day; I thought it only fair to her. And, with the Kileys gone, the chance of discovery was gone with them. I still did not dare say anything of John Starr. That was his own concern.

After the meal, Ox and Red hurried out to ready their gear. When I picked up my hat, Mrs. Lowall came to me and said: "Tod, be careful. Look out for the boys. And, please, keep John out of danger." She looked almost haggard with worry.

"Ma'am, you don't know John St—Stratton very well. But I'll do my best," I told her.

Sunny caught up with me on the porch. I looked at her. She had been subdued all through supper. Now she came close to me, her beautiful face serious.

"Tod, what Mother said—well, she isn't the only one that worries about—about people. I want you to know—well—oh, Tod, I like you better'n anybody I ever met!"

She came up on tiptoe. For the briefest of seconds her soft lips brushed my cheek. Before I could reach for her, she was away, running into the house. I walked toward the corral, touched and warmed. It was the first time since my mother had died that I had known such a caress.

We rode past the house at moonrise, three men well armed, with a packhorse bearing bedrolls, food, and extra ammunition. Our slickers were tied behind our saddles. The Winchesters in the saddle boots were loaded.

The front door opened. I could see Beth and Sunny Lowall silhouetted against the square of yellow lamplight.

"Good luck and God bless you!" Beth called. They were still waving at us as we rode from view.

Ox Pendroy took the lead, for he knew the country well. We had been riding for an hour, northeast along the main trail, when I signaled a stop. By now the moon was high and brilliant, sweeping the long prairie with misty, quivering light, all the shadows pools of impenetrable jet. In the hushed stillness the pounding hoofs of the horse I had heard grew louder. Ox and Red split, moving beside the trail. Near Ox, I edged Prince into the black shadow of a twisted juniper and waited.

The hoofbeats grew uncommonly loud. Then the rider came square into the jaws of our trap. At the last, Red and Ox turned in behind him. I jumped Prince out into the trail, blocking it.

"Hold it, stranger, or we fire!" I called over my pistol sights.

The rider sawed at the bit. The horse reared and slid.

"Whoa, g'dang ye, whoa up!" the man yelled. He curbed his excited mount. "All right, what d'ye want? I've got no gold, no dinero, no wampum. So shoot me and git it over with!"

I rode up to him, laughing, and holstered my pistol. "Not yet for a while, Bart," I said. "Why are you riding hellbent for leather tonight?"

"Why, Tod Morgan, ye young spriggins!" he said, relief in his tone. "So the Injun telegraft was right."

"How's that, old-timer?"

"It's whisperin' the Stranglers are ridin' at sunup. Around Miles, the owlhoot boys, even the reformed ones, is skitterin' off by ones and twos, headin' fer safer climes. The tougher ones, though, aim to jine up with their pals and make a fight outen it. Or so the grapevine says."

"Where's Bent Lowall?"

"Who knows?" Bart said, exasperation in his voice. "The little skunk gimme the go-by last night. I figger he's headin' to warn Kiley and his gang. I aimed to beat him to it. I figger you got till noon, Tod. You don't scrunch them by then, you'll find a nest of yellerjackets."

"The shooting should be over long before then," I told him. "This thing is organized to the last detail, and I think we have plenty of men. You want to join us?"

"It would pleasure me mightily. Only, I got to get on to the ranch and tell Miz Lowall about her nitwit of a son. Then I gotta ride and see Sam ..."

"Sam who?"

"Never you mind Sam who. He ain't no outlaw, anyhow. I'll jest say 'so long' and leave you go about your business. Don't take no wooden nickels nor .44 slugs, boys."

"Try not to, Bart."

"Jest you keep your head down and your tail up, you'll be all right." He spurred his pony onto the trail. His hard dry laughter echoed across the hush of the night.

"Think the renegades will be warned in time?" Beckett asked with some anxiety.

"I doubt it," I said. "It's a long ride out of Miles to Burnt Rock. And as far as Bent Lowall is concerned, the whole thing would be just a rumor. I don't think he'll blow the gag, Red. It would take too much figuring for him."

"Yeah, the dam' dumb kid," Red said. "Still, you can't tell how that frog will jump. But if he's got brains, he sure don't use 'em."

"Anybody that makes a hero outen Shan Kiley ain't got the brains of a lopeared louse, in my book," Ox Pendroy said.

"Well, we'll get our answer at the end of this road," I said. "Let's ride."

At a long, ground-eating lope we rode into the glittering moonlight.

FOURTEEN

As we looked down from the hillside in the thin light of early dawn, the Ingersoll spread didn't seem an easy nut to crack. I hadn't observed all of it the time I was there with Sunny, when the Indian died. There wasn't time. Now I saw that the cabin and store were built like a fort, even to the rifle slots cut in the walls. A log stable beyond the corral looked as solid. The large tent over by the riverbank had been buttressed to half its height with adzed logs.

The outlaws might have been waiting behind those log walls with cocked rifles, but more than likely they had the supreme contempt of their kind for prudence. There were at least a hundred horses in the corral. The outlaws must know, after the McKenzie hanging, that the country was buzzing with wrath. Yet there wasn't a sign of a sentry anywhere. The only sign of human life was a faint wisp of smoke from the stovepipe of the cabin.

"Almost light enough," Grant Stevens said quietly. He leaned forward, staring down at the layout, stroking his heavy beard.

"For straight shooting," John Starr agreed. He looked around at us, frowning a little, "One thing, men. Be sure of your target, then shoot to kill. For these men are sure to resist arrest. They are known killers, possibly barring Ingersoll."

"Wouldn't be no thieves iffen nobody bought the loot," Ox Penroy said.

"I hear Ingersoll is a Harvard graduate," another man said.

"First time I knew they taught hoss stealin' back there."

"He shouldda gone to your school, Starr," Reece Anderson remarked. "He could have took up gunology and triggernometry."

"It would serve him better today than his Greek and Latin," Stevens said. Then, with a cutting sweep of the hand, he commanded silence.

"All right. You all know your assignments. Try to carry them out. We want a clean sweep of this den of rattlers. We want every outlaw killed or captured. Let's go."

The horse holder, trying to look displeased, gathered the reins and led the horses behind the brow of the hill. The men fanned out on foot, with three of them swinging around to hit at the tent building on the bank.

I went straight down the hill with Stevens and Starr. Our trail stood black in the dew-silvered grass. We spread out, walking straight toward the front of the cabin.

A man came out of the front door, carrying a bucket. He saw us, and stood frozen with surprise for a moment. Then he dropped the bucket and turned toward the door.

"Hold it, Ingersoll," Stevens shouted. He motioned with his rifle. "Open that corral gate and let the horses out."

The gate was just beyond the end of the cabin. Ingersoll edged warily over to it, unhooked the barred gate, and swung it partly open. The horses, hungry, crowded close. One slipped through the gap, another, then a stream. They cut between us and Ingersoll. He saw his chance and dashed for the cabin door.

"Halt!" Starr called. "Surrender and you'll get a fair trial."

The man was into the doorway now. He yelled back: "Hell with you! I know your vigilante justice!" He slammed the door. From a slot beside it a rifle began pecking at us. We took cover, prone in the long grass.

Stevens' idea of turning the stolen horses out of danger had backfired on us. Some of them stayed to graze between us and the cabin, despite the noise of gunfire.

Starr said, "Get them out of there, Tod."

I stood up, feeling naked in full view of the cabin rifle slots. I walked swiftly down the hill, trying not to run or flinch, hearing the whine of bullets passing near me. But the fire from the cabin was inaccurate. I got behind the horses, waving my arms and yelling. I managed to spook them, running them clear of the danger area. I went on, then, toward the end of the cabin.

There was hot firing now from the tent beyond. But that was up to the boys assigned to it. I had my own work cut out. I saw, with some surprise, that in their strange blind confidence the criminals had discounted or ignored the possibility of attack from the river side. There were no rifle ports in the blind wall.

But there was a good pile of dry hay. I scratched a lucifer into sputtering flame, kicked a hole in the hay, and dropped the flaming match into it. I stepped back to wait, hearing from inside the building the muffled thud of the firing.

I didn't have long to wait. The logs, desiccated by many blazing Montana summers, caught fire easily. From the burning wall the flames jumped to the roof. The shakes caught. I wiggled backward into position to cover the door, my rifle ready. Yet in spite of the heat and the smoke, gunfire still lanced from the rifle ports. I found myself holding my breath, wondering how flesh and blood could bear it.

Grant Stevens cupped his hands and called, "Put down your arms and come out."

"You want us, come and get us!" a defiant voice yelled in reply.

When the heat was getting hard to bear even where I lay, four men came streaming from the door, firing as they came. I saw one giant figure, his clothes smoldering, firing a pistol with each hand. Jumbo Eiler.

I pumped three bullets into him. He fell like a toppled tree and lay still. That, I thought, will make Pretty Wolf sleep well. I saw the others fall. Warily, we came up on them. Ingersoll, Art Cobb, Flicker Hardy. All dead. The roof came down in a crash of sparks and a wave of overpowering heat. As flame burst, I saw another body inside. We never did learn who it was.

"The boys are having trouble down yonder," Starr said. Bent low, we ran around the cabin, toward the tent. The firing had been hot, pinning our men down. My uncle and I opened up on the canvas, firing fast. Reloading, we waited for return fire. None came.

Starr waved to Cantrell, Adams, and Tabor to advance. Cautiously they came forward, guns ready. We all reached the tent at the same time. Starr burst into it. It was empty. The canvas was ripped and slashed with bullets, and the plank floor was stained with gore, but there was no man, living or dead, inside it.

"We'll take out after 'em," Cantrell muttered.

"He won't get it today," Starr told him. He turned toward the open space where Grant Stevens waited before the embers of the cabin.

"We botched it, Stevens," my uncle reported bitterly.

"Don't take it too hard, John," Stevens said. "We got most of the big bucks." He gestured toward the bodies on the ground.

"Except Rance Kiley," Reece Anderson said. "He was one of the gang at the tent—I saw him duck in as the gunning started."

"He'll have to keep," Stevens said. "Now, men, as you know, I must be in Helena two days from now. I want to tell you that today hasn't ended this thing. It won't end until we have rid the country of these badmen. John Starr here will be in charge. He will harry the gang until the last one is gone or dead. I ask only one thing—let no innocent man suffer for the misdeeds of others."

"We'll go by the list of known criminals, Stevens," my uncle said. "Though I surmise there are few honest men in this section. It must have taken a good many punchers to steal a herd as big as this."

After Stevens rode off to the south, we rounded up the horses, There were 160 head, with almost as many different brands, most of them fine animals. We started them up the trail toward Fort Maginnis and the DHS, where they would be held for their true owners.

"What next?" I asked my uncle.

"We'll help trail this herd to the fort. Best place to start, as far as I can see, with this hot potato Stevens handed me. We've got to start rooting 'em out, Tod."

"I s'pose. But I tell you, I've had a gutful of horses lately," I told him.

"We're being paid, remember?" John Starr said. "In gold."

I scowled and turned into the drifting dust of the herd.

We were a couple miles on our way when we met the most dejected, spavined, stringhalt specimen of crowbait I think I ever saw. A young metis boy was riding it, beating it with a willow switch, digging bare heels into its flanks. But his gain in speed for all the effort expended was exactly nothing. The wreck made its own pace toward us.

As the boy rode up, I recognized the 'breed who had brought me the telegram two days ago. His white blood must have overcome the legendary stoicism of the Indian, for his dark face was lugubrious

"My pony, can I get?" he asked fearfully.

"You see him in there? How can you prove he's yours?"

His face brightened. "Him got red ribbon in mane, blue ribbon in tail. Lilly bit scar across one ear. I can get?"

"Let's go look," Starr said. "How'd you happen to lose him?"

The kid looked down, hanging his head. He scratched the withers of his mount with a toe, but he wouldn't answer.

I laughed. "The kid comes from a long line of champion horse thieves. He just can't admit somebody stole his pony."

"All right, Sancho Panza," my uncle said, laughing. "Go with Tod, and he'll rope out your pony for you."

I eased Prince carefully into the middle of the horse herd. There were several pintos, but only one with the wild calico hide that I remembered the kid's horse had flaunted. Prince cut the pinto out to the side and I dabbed a loop on him. Prince backed and held against the lunges of the little paint.

The kid snatched his hackamore off the crowbait and came running. He walked up the taut rope to the pinto, laid a gentle hand on the horse's nose, and said a few quiet words. The pinto snorted once, then relaxed. He took the hackamore without resistance. The kid jumped to his back, slipped off my lass' rope, and sat real proud, a property owner once more.

"I thank you," he said, white teeth gleaming, sooty eyes sparkling. "You good fellers. Spotted Runner, she's all I'm got. I'm t'ink she's gone for good. I thank you much."

"Forget it, kid," I said. "Keep an eye on him, though, for the Kileys and Burr and a few more are still on the loose. They might snitch him again on you."

"Dam' horse t'iefs," the kid said, spitting. "I'm hope you kill um all. Say, you like catch 'em anudder bunch? Dey steal de Dutchman's horses yesterday, head nort' wit' 'em."

"Another bunch of outlaws? Not Kiley's men?" Starr asked.

"Kiley's men, dey know better'n steal the Dutchman's fine horses. Ever'body know dem horses. Dese men, from Canada maybe, dey don't care. Run twenty head across river las' night."

"How many men were there, son?" Starr asked.

"Mebbe four-five, I'm dunno. Tough poonchers, you bet. Dey say dey cut across to Whoop-Up Trail, sell horses across line, make big money."

"Thanks, kid," my uncle said. We watched as the boy turned the pony with hoofs bunched like a cat, slashed him lightly on the flanks with the switch, and waved as the pinto took out, belly to the ground, for the distant peaks of the Crazies.

"Get Ox and Red and Adams," Starr said. "This is a good chance to break up some of this two-way traffic in stolen horse-flesh. That's one of the main purposes of this cleanup, according to Stevens."

As soon as John Starr had given orders to the remaining men to take the herd on into DHS and wait there, the five of us swept north toward the river, riding hard. If they had crossed the Missouri last night, we would have to trail them through the wild reaches of that vast sea of grass between the Missouri and the Milk. That was the land of Piegan and Blood, of Gros Ventre and Assiniboin. Its faint trails were known to few men. We had our work cut out for us.

We reached the ford where the stolen herd had crossed, the tale of their fording written deep in the baked mud of the shores. Ten yards of swimming water, and we came up dripping on the north back. The trail led north, cutting past Black Butte. Whether they intended to cut west later was hard to guess. But now the tracks led straight for the looming bastions of the Little Rockies.

The outlaws were pushing the Dutchman's prime horses hard. They must have known there would be hot pursuit. If they could cross the line before being overtaken, they would be fairly safe. But we were riding even harder, and without the handicap of loose horses to drive.

We passed their bedground of the night before, then fanned out along the fresher trail of today. The going got rougher. Coulees and washes crisscrossed the slopes. The ground swelled toward the north, and the hills grew steeper. Astonishingly clear in the crystal air, the Little Rockies burst forth from the flat plain, true mountains for all that, pine clad, forbidding. A natural nest for lawless and hunted men.

The trail swept into a cleft between towering walls narrowing into a mere slot in the granite. Starr curbed Roller and held up a hand.

"Good place to get our heads shot off, if they've set an ambush," he said. "Tod, we'll ride in slow. You scout ahead. If we hear gunfire, we'll know you found them."

I didn't like his smile.

"Sure, and come a-running," I said, "after I've got myself shot to dollrags. All right, then. When you find me, just put a cactus bud on my chest and leave me for the wolves."

"We'll tell Sunny you died game," Red Beckett said.

I scowled at him. This humor was too grim for comfort. I rode around the corner of the rock wall, feeling mighty lonesome all by my ownself.

I rode with caution, stopping now and then to scan the the ridges. But I saw no one, and no shot came. Half a mile, three-quarters, and ahead the canyon deepened. Between the almost perpendicular walls, the loam of the trail was sharply cut with horse tracks. There was room only for the narrow trail and a frothing little creek in the confines of the cleft.

I shook my head. It had all the elements of a rat trap. I tied Prince beside the trail. Taking my carbine, I started up the trail on foot. I moved with care and precision, almost feeling my way, for my uncle had taught me how to stalk, and taught me well. I eased around the twists of the canyon, knowing that behind any one there might be an ambush.

Yet it still came as a shock when a rifle slug powdered the rock into dust right in front of my nose and skreed off into space. I was down flat and crabbing backward before the slash a rock splinter had left had even begun to sting. I got a double-bend between me and the marksman before I sat up to dab my bleeding cheek and appraise the situation.

FIFTEEN

THERE WASN'T much I could do. I bellied down beside the small creek, quaffed a good draft of icy water, scrubbed the sweat and dust from face and hands, and took the back trail. I met Starr and the others only half a mile down the trail. Ox Pendroy was leading Prince.

"You see them?" my uncle asked.

"No. Canyon looked about the same as here, a little narrower, maybe. Then some quick-on-the-shoot blew half the rock wall off in front of my nose, and I didn't stay to ask questions."

John Starr rubbed his jaw. "Don't blame you. Well, we've got to root 'em out. Since one man could hold the canyon against a cavalry troop, we'll take to the ridges. Red, you go with me to the right. Adams and Ox, you take the left-hand side. Tod, you'll imitate the cavalry. Keep 'em busy with fire from the canyon. And let's not any of us shoot each other, eh?"

I didn't begrudge them their long climb over the hot bare ridges as I moved back to the corner when I had been stopped, though this time I was more circumspect. I ducked behind some low bushes when I smelled tobacco smoke. The sentry was close. I wriggled closer. And snapped a stick under my elbow.

Luckily, I was on the move at the sound, into the sag of a little wash fronted by a boulder. The guard pumped five shots into the place where I had been as fast as he could work the lever of his rifle. At that, one of the bullets scaled off the top of the boulder, screaming as it keyholed. I hugged the gravel.

I squinted around the corner of the rock and saw movement under a stunted pine fifty yards away. I slammed two shots at it, and ducked. Another gun answered from across the creek. Fortunately, they couldn't get a wide-enough angle at me to produce a dangerous crossfire.

For the next hour, with the sun dropping below the rim of the ridges, I kept them busy. And they kept me hugging the ground. It wasn't fun. The heat and the deerflies nagged at me. The tinkle of the little creek, so close yet so unattainable, was torture for a thirsty man. I threw a shot at each position, ducked back, and waited for the answering fire.

It never came. I waited for another five minutes; then I topped off the magazine of the Winchester, let the hammer down and crouching, made my way through the thin brush to the right. I worked up on the pine where the first fire had come from. When I got to the edge of the cover, I saw that the place was empty.

I stood up, angry at myself, and chagrined at my gullibility. Very likely they were three miles away with the horse herd by now, while I had lain watching the empty mouse hole. I moved up the canyon, in my disgust not even going over to the trail, but slogging through brush and beaver dams on the far side of the creek. I wondered what my uncle's comment would be.

But I had guessed wrong again. Ahead, rifle fire ripped down the ledges. A man yelled. I hurried forward, keeping cover. Around a rock swell, a small basin opened out. From the ridges above it powder smoke puffed even as I watched. I should have known, I thought ruefully. Starr's strategy never fails.

Beyond a thin screen of trees a horse squealed in agony. A man's voice yelled something, defiance in its tone. Then I heard the heavy drumming of hoofbeats. The horse herd had been turned back and was storming toward the gap. Above, from the slopes, the firing grew furious.

I waited, my rifle cocked and ready. A man on a saddled horse led the way. He was lacing his quirt back and forth across his mount, while he rode bent forward like a jockey. As he came bolting through the slot where the canyon narrowed, I fired once.

The horse crossed his legs and pinwheeled. The man sailed through the air, arms and legs spread-eagled, screaming as he went. He lit fair in the trail. He rolled, squalling in terror, seeing the horse herd pounding down upon him. He disappeared under the rush of them. His cries were cut off abruptly. One horse fell. Then they were gone. The downed horse struggling up and limping after the others out of sight around a bend. In the trail lay the dead horse of the outlaw—and a crumpled heap of dark, stained clothing. Nothing moved.

The rifles were silent now. I pushed ahead through the brush, to peer through the screen of trees. Two men stood in a small clearing, their hands in the air. My uncle, Adams, and the two punchers were approaching from either side, rifles ready. I shrilled the woodchuck whistle that Starr knew, and after a moment's wait I stepped out from the trees.

"Fan them, Tod," Starr ordered.

I laid rifle and pistol on a convenient rock and, unarmed, moved up behind the men. I stripped them of pistol belts, found a holdout gun in the armpit of one, a Green River knife in a neck sheath, a steel toothpick in the slack of a boot. All on the older man. The younger, not much more than a kid, was clean. Satisfied, I stepped back, the acrid sweat of the fear they emanated strong in my nostrils. I noticed the great damp half-moons under their armpits.

"They're stripped," I said.

Starr moved in front of the two, handing me his rifle. He hooked his thumbs through his cartridge belt.

"Lower your hands," he told them. "Now, who are you?"

One of them was tall, whiskered, unshorn, wild of eye and broken of teeth. He stared off at the mountaintop, as if not caring about his surroundings. I've caged catamounts with the same look.

The kid was slight, wizened of face, and not more than six-teen at most. A bullet graze on one shoulder still seeped scarlet.

"My name's Cordova," he said. "This is Jack Stringman. We was jest ridin' north and fell in with them other fellers."

Just then there was a little commotion. Adams came out of the brush, prodding a short, potgutted man who had a broken nose and a crazy slash of scar across one cheek.

"So they smoked you out, Cully!" the tall outlaw said, with satisfaction. Then, hardly moving his lips, he turned such a stream of blasphemy and invective on Cully that the man cringed.

Starr took a step forward and smashed Stringman across the mouth with the back of his hand. "Shut up!" he said.

Stringman subsided, a bright bead of blood forming on his lower lip. He looked back to the mountaintop.

"Another one dead in the brush," Adams said.

"And another yonder down the trail," I added.

"All right, that's the bunch. You men have any messages to write, any prayers to pray, get it done. I'll give you ten minutes.

Cully's face crumpled like wet dough. Stringman never moved. The boy flinched as if struck with a lash.

Adams said it for us. "The kid too, Starr?"

My uncle bit his lip and looked at the boy.

"First horses you ever stole?" he asked.

The boy stared at him with agony in his eyes. Then he shook his head slowly. "No. But I never..."

"There's your answer, Adams," Starr said.

With the stupidity of his kind, Cully thought he saw a way out.

"I never stole no horses before," he said eagerly. "Not really now, neither. I jest happened to be ridin' north and—"

"And fell in with them. I know," John Starr said. "You know anybody ever did steal any horses, Cully?"

"Sure, Stringman there, and the kid, and him down the trail, Lott Hammer. But I never did."

"Of course not. Who did they work for, then?"

"Why, their own selves. They used to work for Rance Kiley, but Stringman had a run-in with Jumbo Eiler, and him and the kid and Lott pulled out. They joined the Injun back there in the brush, then decided to raid the Dutchman and sell his good hosses acrost the line. Or so they say. Me, I jest fell in with them."

"Maybe they told you more," Starr said. "Who else worked for Kiley? Anybody named Pendroy? Or Beckett? Or Benton Lowall?"

"Pendroy and Beckett? Them two dam' fools wouldn't know enough to pick up a double eagle iff'n it was layin' right under their nose. The Lowall kid, he ain't been on no raids, they say, but Shan Kiley's got him where he wants him. He aims to get aholt of the kid's short hair and end up with the Lazy L herd. And that little sassy gal, Lowall's sister. He's a sly one, that Shan."

"I see, Cully. Well, you've got five minutes left. Boys, get your ropes over a strong cottonwood limb. Let's get the work over and head for home."

"What you gonna do?" Cully cried in alarm.

"Hang you," Starr said. "You knew the penalty, Cully. This is the payment for those high old times in Miles and Fort Benton, for the brag and the bluster, and the men you killed in dry gulches."

"But I thought—" Cully wailed.

"Shut your dam' fat mouth," Stringman snarled. "The man is right. You allus was a tallow gut. But now try to take your medicine like a man."

Ox and Red rode upstream, looking for a suitable gallows tree. Adams held the prisoners under his gun. John Starr walked off a little distance, his head bowed, his shoulders slumped.

I looked at young Cordova. I felt a desperate pity for the kid. You could tell by the look of him he had never had a decent chance. And there was a spark of courage in him that appealed to me. Except for Starr, I thought, I might have gone down the same trail as this kid two years ago. Surely he could be merciful to one so young.

I walked over to my uncle.

"That Cordova kid—he's awful young. Likely didn't know any better, or have a chance to live right. Can't we give him a horse and run him toward the border, after the—the hanging of the other two?"

Starr looked at me. He turned away then, without speaking, and walked slowly through the grass in the long twilight for fifty yards, a hundred. He stopped, stood quiet. Then he turned and came back.

If ever I saw the shadow of inner agony on a man's face, it was on the face of John Starr. He put a hand on my shoulder. His voice was low and torn with emotion.

"Tod, Tod, forgive me. But Cordova has to hang," he said.

"Why, John, why?" I cried. "He's so *damn'* young. With a scare like this, he'll be a good citizen; I'd bet on it."

"Tod, many years ago in Missouri a young lad was captured during a guerrilla raid. Because of his youth, he went free, instead of hanging, like the others. Because of him, young Cordova must hang." He paused, his face bleak. "That young bandit, Tod, was Tug Rondout."

I began to argue. But I saw the granite determination on Starr's face, and desisted. Anger rose in me.

"I thought you told me that ghost was laid for good," I said bitterly.

"God help me, I thought it was," John Starr said. "But when I remember ... Tod, the boy hangs."

Stringman died bravely, almost uncaring. Cully blubbered and fought, still seeking a way out when Red Beckett quirted the unsaddled horse from under him.

The kid was last, brave enough, apathetic even. He looked young and woebegone, the noose around his neck.

"Give him a chance, Uncle John," I pleaded. "What will Beth think?"

"A man acts according to his rights, Tod," Starr said, his voice flat and cold. "Red, get it over with."

The quirt swung, and it was ended.

I was still sullen and angry as we rode south, the short, unpleasant chore of burial completed. When the trail widened, I rode up alongside Starr.

"I can't understand you, John. Is everything black and white to you, with no shade of gray? I wonder how you would have made answer if that had been Bent Lowall back there."

He looked at me sternly, the signs of suffering still on his lean face.

"Tod," he said, "you can't understand that there are forces in a man which can tear him apart, make him go against his own best interests, make him sacrifice all he holds dear for a principle. The heart of a man, or a woman, is a secret and fathomless thing. Until you know what that means, don't measure me with your callow judgments. Don't ask me questions which haven't any answer."

I looked at him, and saw death in his eyes. Shaken, I dropped back to ride alone.

SIXTEEN

"YOU'RE JOHN STARR? John Starr..."

Beth Lowall's voice caught a little. I saw shocked disbelief on her face. She shook her head, looking squarely at him. Then, slowly, her lips parted in a smile. She came over to my uncle and placed both hands on his arms.

"Why, I don't know any reason to think less of you, John. I've always heard that John Starr worked only with the law. I suppose it was the shock of learning you were not what you seemed."

"I'm not an angel," Starr said gently. "I've killed men in my time. And men have tried to kill me."

"Will there be an end to that, John?" she asked.

"That is my hope," he said gravely. "But it must go on for a while." Tersely, he told her of the pursuit and execution of the horse thieves. He spoke bluntly, not even concealing how young the boy Cordova had been.

She gasped. "Oh, dear God, no. You hanged a—child?"

"I had no choice, Beth," Starr said.

"But what if it had been Benton?"

He took her hand in his. "I'd try to save him, Beth. His first offense..."

"But what of the others? You aren't the only one wreaking justice on these outlaws. If my son happened to be in bad company when the vigilantes overtook them, he'd die with them, wouldn't he?"

"I'm afraid so."

"Then we *must* find him. You swear that he hasn't been hurt, John? That you don't know where Benton is?"

"I swear it," Starr said. "Last I heard, he was in Miles City, and Bart Stoker had come back here."

"And has gone again, on his own mysterious business," Beth told him. "Benton must have heard the news of the raids by now," she said distractedly. "If I know him, he'll have some ill-advised project afoot to rescue Shan Kiley. He'll get himself killed, John! We must find him immediately." She turned to me, anguish in her eyes. "Tod, John doesn't need you for the rest of this business. Will you ride my son down and bring him to safety?"

I shot a glance at Starr. Almost imperceptibly he nodded.

"Sure I'll go, Mrs. Lowall," I said. "Give me time for a bait of grub and a change of horses."

Starr and I studied the map as I gulped the food Mrs. Ledger had set out for me. My uncle drew a line along the map.

"Heading this way from Miles, he'd pass here and here. Looks like your best bet for a shot in the dark, Tod, is this post here, about twenty miles below Burnt Rock. Man named Sam Lecky runs it. If you don't get a lead there, keep working east." He folded the map and thrust it into my pocket. "I have a feeling it's a wild-goose chase, son," he said. "But be careful every minute. The country is still buzzing with snakes like the Kileys. And if you find the boy, mind how you handle him. You know what it means—to all of us."

"Before I could answer, Mrs. Lowall came into the room with Sunny following her. Both were flushed with anger, and both had traces of tears on their faces.

"Are you ready, Tod?" Sunny asked quietly. I saw then that she was wearing her outlandish divided skirt and that around her waist she wore cartridge belt and holster, with a businesslike .38 in the leather.

"It seems you'll have company whether you will or no, Tod," Mrs. Lowall said, tight-lipped. "No argument seems to prevail with this stubborn young fool. She cares nothing for the danger."

"Mother, I know the country, every foot of it, and Tod does not. And I've always been able to handle Benton," Sunny said, defiantly.

"Well, I trust Tod," Mrs. Lowall said. "But I hope you don't have cause to regret this day, Sunny. Tod, take good care of her."

I gulped hard. "Dam' if I won't try," I said.

I didn't cotton to the thought of dragging a young female clean across Montana Territory, with lead flying. But at the same time I felt excitement at the thought of traveling alone with Sunny.

Mrs. Ledger, who had been rummaging in the pantry, brought out a canvas sack and plunked it on the table. She looked at me with pursed lips. "Long's the two of ye is ridin' to hell, might as well have suthin' t' eat on the way." She looked Sunny up and down. "That's an ungodly outfit to travel in," she added, her disdain monumental.

At the corral I caught up Blackie, the fine horse I had ridden on the night of the raid on Silver Spring. I watched Sunny, not offering advice. But I was pleased when she picked a big raw-boned dun horse with a lantern jaw but with a sure, steady gait.

Sunny rode up beside me when we were out of sight of the ranch. "I s'pose you're madder'n hops at me," she said.

"No use in that," I told her. "But I mean it when I say I don't like the added risk of having you along. Suppose something happens to me? These aren't Sunday-school kids, Sunny. They catch you alone, they'll have you praying for death before they're through with you. I saw an Indian girl once, after a gang like this had used and broken her. I never want to see the like again."

She went pale under her tan. "Never mind that, Tod. I want to save my brother."

"Sunny, you're lying to me," I said. "You're not that close to Bent. This concern for his safety sounds put on to me."

"It's for Mom's sake. Sure, she knows Bent's faults, but she loves him just the same. If he got hurt or killed, I'd feel badly—after all, he *is* my brother. But Mom would go to pieces.

"And the rest of it?"

For answer, she stood up in the stirrups, swinging her body to look off at the blue haze of the Little Rockies far away across the river. She swept her gaze around the full horizon. As if relieved of a doubt, she dropped back into the leather.

"Tod, I'm eighteen. I've lived on this frontier in the midst of outlaws and renegades, through battle and murder and sudden death. And I might as well have been a spinster lady in Boston. Men have made and are making history here. I sit at Lazy L and sew and bake and mend like a good little girl, while the world spins around me. Today I couldn't stand it a minute longer. For once I want to see things and do things and know things—I want to be a part of this dangerous world. Can you understand that?"

"Seems a funny way for a lady to act," I said.

"Tod Morgan, I'm damned sick and tired of being a lady!" she flared.

"Sunny!" I said, shocked at her language. But I did under-stand. I realized I had been given a glimpse of the passionate inner heart of this girl of the frontier.

We were still riding when the sun dropped behind the ser-rated ridge of the distant Rockies. Then the world was bathed in a flush of salmon and rose-gold. I felt the cool fingers of the night breeze on my face, and the day's heat dropped away. The stirring air brought with it the scent of sage and dust, of balm of Gilead and sun-warmed juniper.

I sat a little straighter in the saddle. I hadn't known until now how bone-weary I was. I was young and tough and well nigh indestructible, but I had had only about five hours' sleep in the last sixty. And beyond the physical fatigue of hard, long riding, there was the mental and emotional strain of pursuit and death and destruction. As far as I was concerned, Bent Lowall could go to hell his own way for another day.

But I didn't say anything. Lecky's post was miles away. I was too proud to admit that I was bushed, for Sunny was still riding straight and alert, seemingly fresh. I scrounged around in the saddle, trying to find a comfortable position. Streamers of coral and violet and magenta bannered down the sky, faded into deep purple, and fled before the coming darkness. We rode on.

Finally Sunny said, "Tod, it's getting dark."

"It will get darker before the moon comes up," I said curtly.

"What's the matter with you?" she asked sharply. "You don't have to baby me. I've lived outdoors as much as you. I can ride and camp and even trail as good as most men. Why don't you try to forget that I'm a girl?"

"That's just it—I can't," I said.

She rode up closer beside me. "Tod, you're just tired and cranky. I'll try to keep from delaying you—and I'll not ask for any special favors.

"That's fine. Except that I'm not a wooden Indian, Sunny. I don't know how long I can play the gentleman."

"As long as it's necessary!" she snapped. "I'm not a dance-hall hussy, and you know it."

Quick anger rose in me. How can a girl devil a man so, and still turn things so that the blame is on him?

She must have sensed my hurt. She edged her horse close to mine, reached over and took my hand. "I'm sorry, Tod," she said softly. "But I'm afraid I'm human too. I don't understand all these feelings stirring in me. Maybe—maybe I *am* a hussy. Maybe what I said was just whistling in the dark."

"All right, kid," I said. "We'll call a truce."

The moon was just skimming the far buttes when we came to the slant that led down to the river bottoms. Below, glittering through the trees, we saw a small campfire. Nearby lamplight made a golden square of a cabin window.

"Hold the horses, Sunny," I directed. "I'll take a turn down there on foot. If there's trouble, turn Blackie loose and head for help as hard as you can cut. You hear?"

"All right, Tod," she said humbly. "Only, I've been around a pretty salty bunch of men all my life. They've taught me to shoot, and shoot straight. So I might change my mind about riding."

"All right, all right," I said laughing a little. "Only, when I come back, don't plug me first and ask questions later."

Lecky's post was as much like the one at Burnt Rock as two peas in a pod, except that this one was smaller. No one challenged me as I came around the end of the cabin in the moonlight. With gun in hand, I edged across the packed dirt to the cabin door. I eased the latch free, set my shoulder against the planks, and thrust it open, swinging my pistol to cover whoever might be inside.

Two men looked up from their checker game under the lamp. One was hatchet-faced, with a scraggle of dirty whiskers and one empty eye socket. The other was Bart Stoker.

"Why, Tod, boy," Bart exclaimed. "What in Tophet you doing here?"

"Hunting for young Lowall. Seen anything of him?"

"Neither hide nor hair nor tracks in the tall timber. Tod, this here's Sam Lecky. Sam, meet a young heller with lightnin' in his shootin' hand—Tod Morgan."

"Pleased, Morgan, right pleased," Lecky said, putting out a corded hand. "What's young Lowall done? I figgered he would get hisself in trouble sooner or later. Morgan, that kid's been through here more'n onst. Nobody tells him nothin'. He knows it all and he's bound and determined he's gonna be a big bold badman. I alluz figgered he'd make if, too, if somebody didn't kill him dead first."

"He's still clear, far as I know," I told him. "But his mother's worried about him. If you see him, fan his butt back to Lazy L, will you?"

"Take a rawhide quirt to him, that's what," Stoker said. "That boy's got bad blood in him, Tod. And Beth Lowall such a fine woman. Ain't life funny?"

"It sure is. But why are you here, Bart? You know what's happening across the Territory. Yet you hole up with a man who is on the list as a buyer of stolen beef and horseflesh, and whose layout is a known rendezvous for outlaws."

"Sam Lecky is my friend," Bart said simply. "An' he don't deserve the sharp edge of your tongue, nuther. What he did—an' I don't say it were all lawful—he had to do. It warn't from choice. You live alongside the owlhoot trail, Tod, you do lots of things you don't like if you want to keep the breath in your body."

"You still didn't tell me why you're here."

"I got the latest news about the raids, and I come to warn Sam here that things ain't safe. He's likely to git it from either side. So fur I cain't convince him he ought to leave. But I got him weakenin'. I beat him another couple dozen games of checkers, I think we'll saddle up and pull out."

"What about the Indians down by the corral?"

"Crows. A small bunch headin' for Canady. Somebody told 'em the missing buffler are running the prairies far north. They're heading for a hunt, for all hell cain't convince 'em it ain't true. Dam' shame, too."

"Sure. Only, all the way up and all the way back—if they come back—they'll live off DHS and Milliron and Fergus beef. Plus snitching every loose pony they come across. Why don't they stay on the reservation?"

"Agent is a bad man, they say," Lecky told me. "Govament beef too pore to eat."

"And they might not be far wrong. Well, the Mounties can worry about 'em. But the country's in a damned nasty mood. If

I were you, Lecky, I'd beat my shadow over the hill when the sun comes up tomorrow. Get clean out of the country for a long spell."

"I s'pose you're right," Lecky grumbled. "But I sure hate to leave this post I worked hard to build up. An' it's fine country, too—barrin' the heat in the summer an' the cold in the winter, and mosquitoes and flies and rattlers, and gunmen on the dodge in between times. But I might bring myself to do it, seein' as a man only has one neck to do him all his life."

"It might save it," I said. "Bart, try to get him moving. And get out yourself. There are plenty of renegades still loose. The word is out that you helped the association."

"We'll skedaddle tomorrow, or maybe the next day," he said, grinning. "Take keer of yourself, son."

I shook hands with the two old-timers, and went out. Before I pulled the door shut behind me they were already poring over their checker game in the smoky lamplight.

Outside, I debated checking on the Indian lodges. But there was no reason for Lecky to lie, nor for Bart to confirm it. I watched the quiet figures around the campfire for a minute, then turned away up the hill.

Sunny challenged me softly, keeping concealed until I answered. When I joined her, she asked, "No sign of Bent?"

"None. Bart Stoker is there with Lecky. And a little bunch of Crows on the hunting trail. They haven't seen Bent. You want to lodge there for the night?"

She gave a little cry of dismay. "I know those posts, Tod. They're alive with vermin. No thanks. Shall we ride the east trail a ways and find a spot to camp?"

"Fine with me. I'm about at the end of my rope. Lead on." At the top of the hill she turned the dun southeast. I let Blackie follow. My chin dropped to my chest, and I half slept.

SEVENTEEN

"TOD! TOD! WAKE UP! Is this far enough?"

At Sunny's cry, I rubbed eyes gritty with sand. It was hard to distinguish objects in the waning moonlight, but I could see that we were in a wide coulee.

"All right for a dry camp," I said.

"Get off your horse, then," she said.

I swung off Blackie, and came wide awake as I went knee deep into cold wet muck. I struggled to dry land, my boots making heavy sucking sounds as I pulled them free. I stamped on the turf, trying to shake off the clinging mud.

"You little devil, you did that on purpose!" I accused.

"You've been sound asleep for ten miles," she said, chuckling. "I had to wake you up some way. This is a spring called Deer Lick, near the main trail. We ought to be able to hear any rider going by."

"I doubt if I'd hear the trump of Gabriel tonight," I said, unstrapping my bedroll. "Besides, your brother must know that the night trails aren't safe even for honest men. I misdoubt he'd ride at night."

"Do you want something to eat? Mrs. Ledger's sandwiches will make a snack."

"I'll wait for morning."

I spread Sunny's bedroll, and then, at a little distance, my own. I dug a hole for my hip, set my saddle for a pillow, pulled off my boots, and put gunbelt and holster close to my hand. I was under blanket and tarp while Sunny was still stirring around.

I started to tell her something but fell asleep before the words came.

A slight noise brought me awake. Forcing one eye open, I saw it was gray dawn. Turning my head slowly as the sound came again, I slid my hand to the cold butt of my pistol. Then I breathed easier.

It was a buck deer, come to drink from the slough below the spring. He raised his head from the water, the jeweled drops sprinkling from his muzzle. He seemed uneasy, but he drank again. Satisfied, he snorted softly, then minced away from the pond with stiff, almost soundless steps, and vanished.

I turned to look for Sunny. In the sharp air, she had slid entirely out of sight beneath the covers. I sat up, shivering a little. I pulled on my boots, slid into my vest, and stood up. I was buckling on my cartridge belt when I looked at Sunny's bed once more. My mouth went dry with panic.

Sunny's body was a long mound under the blanket and tarp. And there, no doubt seeking warmth against the night chill, lay the thick gray and dirty tan coils of a big rattler close against it. Sluggish now, and not immediately dangerous, he still might coil and strike if the girl awakened and thrust her face or a hand from the bedding. I dared not call to warn her.

I moved toward the head of the bedroll. I would have to fire down the length of her body to avoid hitting her. I cocked the gun and moved closer. Feeling the slight vibration, the evil triangular head came up a little. Reaching down for a small stone, I tossed it square into the thick, ugly body.

The rattler twisted instantly into a coil. The head drew back like a poised lance, and the tail blurred with the dried-pea buzz of warning. I fired, one shot blasting the wicked head to pulp, the second slamming the squirming body away from the tarp. The sounds of the shots were startlingly loud in the still of the morning.

Sunny exploded out of the rumpled bed to stare wide-eyed at the smoking revolver. As she turned to discover the target, she saw the still writhing body of the snake, and gave a cry of horror. She ran to me, and I caught her tight in my arms. She was shaking with fright and shock. Gradually I felt her grow calm. She pushed herself away.

Only then did both of us realize that she wore no blouse. She flung her arms up in front of her, covering what she could of the lovely white flesh of shoulder and bosom. I saw a deep V of tan against the creamy skin, the neckline of her blouse. I forced myself to turn away.

Her face was still flaming with embarrassment when I turned around as, fully dressed, she said, "All right, Tod." I must have looked uncomfortable, for suddenly she began to laugh. She put a hand on my arm.

"And I told you I wasn't a hussy, Tod," she said. "But, then, I've never had a rattlesnake in my bed before!"

We had breakfast and then rode east. The cool of the morning soon evaporated under the searing July sun. We talked little as we rode through the heat and the glare, the small episode of that morning seeming to place constraint between us.

The country seemed quiet. The cattle were seeking the sparse brush of the coulee bottoms for what little shade it could provide. Again we saw a herd of woolies dotting a hillside above the trail, though there was no sign of camp wagon or herder or dogs. I had the feeling that the whole country was holding its breath, like the hushed quiet before a line storm. Even the cloudless, brassy sky seemed ominous.

We came at midday to a junction of three roads. One led north toward Circle and Fort Buford, one straight ahead into the maco sicca and, beyond it, the Little Missouri; and one turned right toward Miles City and the railroad. Sunny studied the ground long, then turned to stare into the heat-warped blue of the horizon.

"Let's ride north," she said at last.

It was as likely a way as any, I thought. Though I was sure now that we had missed Benton Lowall, I had little stomach for turning back into the turmoil of the Basin. So we rode steadily on, once more to meet the big river.

That night we stayed at Rocking R, where the womenfolk made much of Sunny; they saw a strange white woman about once in a coon's age. They cast shocked and surreptitous glances at her divided skirt. I overheard them saying how unwomanly it was. But even as they talked, they got out cloth and thread and scissors to duplicate it.

Around noon we struck another crossroads trading post, near Poplar Agency. We tied our horses to the hitch rail and went in. The long room was cool after the blaze of sun, but there was no storekeeper to be seen.

"Anybody home?" I called.

Bedsprings creaked, and from an inner room came a long, lean man, rubbing his eyes and combing his hair and whiskers with the spread fingers of his hand.

"Why, howdy," he said, his stretched smile showing a complete lack of teeth in the upper jaw. "Name's Peterson. Kin I do suthin' fer ye and the young lady?"

"A place where she can freshen up a bit. As for me, a basin of water and a bar of soap. Then a bait for the horses, and I hope you have something cool to drink."

"Why, wouldn't surprise me a mite iffen I couldn't meet that whole order," he said, grinning. "Come with me, missis." He led Sunny inside his living quarters and then came back. While I was snuffling and snorting in soapy water at an outside bench, he fed the horses. When I returned, Sunny stood by the counter, shining and refreshed. She smiled at me.

On the counter was a snack of crackers, cheese, pickles, canned fruit, and jam. And, miracle of miracles, a bottle of sarsaparilla and one of lager beer, beady with moisture.

I downed half my bottle at a gulp. "Peterson, you're a Scandinavian angel," I said sincerely. "How do you produce ice-cold beer in the middle of a wilderness?"

"Well, you might think I'm a funny critcher, but I near died of sunstroke onst, down by Independence. Since then seems like the heat floors me somethin' awful. So when I built here, I dug me a tremenjus big icehouse, like a root cellar. Come January, I cut me enough forty-below ice off'n the pond to fill 'er, and she lasts me all summer. Keeps my meat and grub sweet and fresh and my lager cold. Pretty hard to beat."

As I drained the last of the brew, he flicked the cap off another bottle.

"You do well to keep ice at all in this weather, mister," I told him. "It's sure hot enough."

"You're talkin' about ordinary ice, man. Mine is forty-below ice. Why, you cain't hardly melt 'er a-tall. Like today, I put a cake of her alongside the house, whistle up a breeze, and that there chunk of forty-below ice will keep the whole shebang right cool fer a day and a half, two days. Notice how 'tis in here? On top o' that, the place where that cake set will be so cold fer a week she'd freeze the gizzard out'n a live chicken!"

He cackled, slapping his thigh, and we laughed with him.

When we finished lunch, I paid him. "Thanks for your kindness, Mr. Peterson," I said. "One more thing—we're looking for this young lady's brother. Man in his early twenties, dark, slim built. Seen a man like that lately?"

He cocked his head, tugged at his whiskers. "Might be they call him 'Bent'?"

"That's him!" I said. "When was he here?"

He was very busy all of a sudden. Over his shoulder, he said, "Yestidday, I guess."

"Was he alone?" I persisted.

He turned, placed his two hands flat on the counter.

"Mister, get this straight. This is tough country and I know it. Man stays alive longer by keepin' his mouth shet."

I stared at him. "You know dam' well the big cleanup is on. If you help us, you won't have to worry about the owlhoot tribe.

You play your own game, some night a bunch of riders with a rope…"

"My God, no, mister, not that!" he cried.

I didn't like it, but I was in a hurry. "All right, tell me the truth, then."

"Well, the two of 'em was something liquored. Fust, they told me the news."

"Who was the other man? And what news?"

" 'Nother young feller, dark-complected, hard-lookin'. A twisty white scar over his right eye."

"Shan Kiley!" Sunny exclaimed.

"Mebbe. Anyhow, they was braggin' a little about how a bunch of outlaws dodged the vigilantes at Burnt Rock. They hid out until dark and then made rafts outen old logs and floated down the river whilst the vigilantes was lookin' for 'em on the trails. Then they landed by Poplar Agency, an' accounted for the wounds of some of 'em by tellin' the agent a tale of bein' jumped by renegade Blackfoot."

"What happened then?"

"The agent fed 'em, bound up their wounds and, like the Bible says, was trying to outfit 'em when they come a telly-graft from the colonel at Fort Maginnis sayin' look out for 'em. So the agent thrun them all in the calaboose. There's a depitty U.S. marshal comin' from Maginnis to take 'em there. Or so these two fellers said."

"Then what?"

"The older one, the man you called Shan, he was ory-eyed. They wasn't talkin' loud, but I heard a leetle now and then. 'It's my did's neck,' Shan says. 'The Crossing's the place to do it.' The younger one argues with him. 'All right, yellerback, git over to the Agency and warn the swaddies, then,' Shan told him. The young one asked somethin' I didn't ketch. 'Sure I mean it,' Shan says. 'It's them that put Dad in this jam, damn 'em.' S'cuse the cussin', ma'am, but that's what he said."

"Sure he said Lecky's?" I asked.

"That's right. Say, you don't s'pose he meant ole Sam Lecky, do you, runs the backwoods post up the river?"

"You just think of that?" I asked.

His glance slid away from mine. Then he moved his hands in a helpless gesture. He was right, I suppose. What could he have done? I shook my head.

"Come on, Sunny," I said. "Let's ride."

I put Blackie to a fast pace. That had been yesterday. The chance was that whatever deviltry Kiley intended had been done by now. And by now Benton Lowall was in deep enough to bring him to his death with the others—death at the hands of John Starr, the Vigilantes—and me. I didn't like it. I held to the faint hope that Bent had been smart enough to avoid trouble.

We rode hard, without rest and without talk. Still, the sunset was flaring across a stippled sky when we rode up to the edge of the clearing where Lecky's store stood. I held my hand out flat to stop Sunny. We sat there, listening.

There was no sound, not even the mewing cry of the night-hawks. The Indian lodges were gone from the open strip below the corral. There wasn't any light in the store, and no smoke was wisping from the stovepipe. We rode down to it.

The door was open. I swung down and went in. The stock was strewn around, and bottles lay broken on the plank floor. A case of cartridges was smashed open on the counter; several boxes had been taken, and another lay spilling shiny brass cylinders over the wood.

I walked out, paused uncertainly, then skirted the cabin.

EIGHTEEN

"SUNNY, STAY BACK!" I called. "Don't—"

But she had been right on my heels.

"What is it, Tod? Oh, no. Dear God, no!" she cried. She turned away, burying her face in her hands.

Sickness surged up in me, but I had to climb the corral bars and, with my knife, saw at first one, then the other of the ropes hanging from the high crossbar. When the bodies had thudded into the dust beneath, I climbed down. Gently, I turned them over.

They were swollen by the day's heat, the faces empurpled by the throes of strangulation. Sam Lecky, who hadn't heeded, fast enough, the warning that had been given him. And Bart Stoker, the grand old man who had stood on his own feet and spat in the eye of the outlaws once too often.

"Poor old Bart!" Sunny said, her voice trembling. "But who would do such a thing, Tod?"

I plucked a crudely lettered sign from the gatepost.

"Here's your answer, kid," I said gruffly. She peered close at it in the gathering dusk.

TO HELL WITH YOU STRANGLERS AND YOUR SPIES

"Shan Kiley, you think? And—and Bent?"

I shrugged. "All I know is what Peterson said," I told her.

"Tod, this will kill Mother, if Bent was in on it."

"I don't know, Sunny; I don't know."

We went into the store. I lighted a lamp and hunted around to find a shovel. Sunny reached into the case and took out its mate.

"Stay here," I told her. "You don't have to help."

"Bart Stoker was my friend," she said simply.

In that moment I was for the first time sure that I loved Sunny Lowall.

The earth of Montana does not yield easily. It resisted grudgingly on the little knoll above the cabin where we dug the double grave. In the end, by lantern light, what we had dug was neither wide nor deep, but it would serve. It would discourage the coyotes, at least.

Wrapped in tarpaulin, the two bodies were placed in the grave. Even as Sunny tearfully recited the Twenty-third Psalm, I piled the dirt back and mounded it up. I drove the two shovel blades deep into the earth at the head. A marker must wait for another day.

We could, I suppose, have stayed the night in the store, but we hardly thought of it. It is only human, I think, to flee the place of death. We went to our horses.

"Kiley must plan a rendezvous with his remaining friends," I told Sunny as we mounted. "Since we don't know where, we've got to ride to the Crossing and warn the soldiers. You know the trail well enough to make a few more miles in the dark?"

"I think so. I'd risk anything to get 'way off from here."

"Because our horses were as weary as we were, we didn't push them. The river trail was a dark tunnel in the starlight. Mosquitoes deviled us in clouds, so we rode with neckerchiefs pulled up around our faces.

At a little creek, Sunny said: "I can't stand any more of this. Let's find higher ground and make camp."

In the pitch black she found a narrow trail, followed it, and came out on a breeze-swept height above the creek. We made camp, using dried grass for mattresses. The horses were hobbled and turned out. We drank cold water and munched crackers for a meager meal. Then we turned in.

Sunny must have remembered the rattlesnake, for, disregarding propriety, she made her bed so close to mine I could hear her soft breathing. There was a stir of excitement in me, yet I was so dog-tired, so torn by the wild events of the last few days, that I could not even talk to her. As I turned so that I could look at the pale glow of her face in the starlight, I felt a wave of tenderness for her.

We started out early the next morning, following the river trail. It twisted among chokecherry and alder, serviceberry and hawthorn, hardly more than a deer trail. Yet always before us were the day-old tracks of two horses. I rode with my Winchester across my thighs, my eye scanning the trail for possible ambush. At the end of a long steep grade we came out of the brush into the open, and stopped to breathe the horses.

Here the air was sharp and clear, and there were no mosquitoes. Far across the river the tilted planes of the Little Rockies blurred in the heat waves. On the flats dust devils formed and danced and broke, only to spring up in new spirals in another place.

My horse's head jerked up. I listened.

"Riders coming," I said. "Let's get off the trail."

Just up the track a great shoulder of rock protruded. We swung behind it, pushing through the scant brush. We were only half concealed, but we were above the trail. As I jacked a shell into the chamber of the Winchester, I heard Sunny's light carbine click as she readied it. We waited.

Then we lowered out guns in relief. John Starr came riding in the lead. Behind him were Taylor, Anderson, Paterson, and Adams, in the rear a group of three—Ox Pendroy, Red Beckett and, graceful on her sidesaddle, Beth Lowall. I hailed them.

John Starr pulled Roller up so fast the big horse slid in the gravel. As the others milled to a stop, we rode down into the trail.

"Sunny!" Beth Lowall exclaimed. "Any news of Benton?"

Sunny glanced at me. Then she said: "No, Mother. But we're sure he's safe."

"Thank God," Mrs. Lowall said, her heart in her voice. She rode close to her daughter, put an arm around her shoulders, and hugged her.

"Learn anything, Tod?" Starr asked quietly.

In a low voice I told him of the events of the last three days. When I came to the brutal killing of Lecky and Bart Stoker, my uncle scowled, and cursed under his breath. But he did not interrupt.

"So they were still heading toward Burnt Rock last night," I concluded. "Where they will round up their rescue party, or where they will strike, I didn't learn. But young Kiley seems to have big ideas."

"That's why we're riding," Starr said. "We're afraid the outlaws will intercept Marshal Fiscel and his party at Burnt Rock ford, kill the officers, and free the prisoners. And Rance Kiley is one of the prisoners."

"Well, Burnt Rock is only a few miles from here," I said. "Let's get there first."

As the group of riders strung out, I ranged my horse alongside Mrs. Lowall's. "How come you're here, ma'am?" I asked.

"I couldn't stay home, not knowing about Benton," she said, "John objected strenuously, but I had to come. Tell me, Tod, my son is in trouble, isn't he? Bad trouble?"

When I met her eyes I knew there was no use lying.

"That's right, Mrs. Lowall. But we don't know just how bad."

"Oh, the fool! Tod, promise me—if there is anything that you can in honor do for Benton, will you do it?"

"You have my promise, Mrs. Lowall," I said. "Though he hasn't made it easy for anyone to help."

We came into Burnt Rock shortly thereafter. The charred logs of the cabins stood undisturbed. Something had been digging at one of the mounds of earth on the hill, and the horses shied a little. Beyond the corral was a shady clearing, long of grass, and windswept enough to be free of mosquitoes.

To one tired from long riding, the grass was pleasantly soft. And I did full justice to our meal, for rations had been less than meager for Sunny and me in the last two days. Because Starr did not put me on lookout duty, after eating I dozed for a little, only to be wakened by Sunny's footsteps in the grass near me.

"Come down by the river," she said.

From the cutbank above the ford, we looked down on the Missouri, wide and quiet here, yellow-green in the shallows, dark green in the depths. It was much tamer than it was a few weeks ago when I first saw it.

I jerked up my head. "That's funny. I could swear I heard a train whistle. Bronc stomping must have addled my brains."

Sunny laughed. "You mean you never heard a steamboat whistle? Watch that bend below, then. You'll see something that's mighty rare here on the upper river. Now and then there's a packet from St. Louis to Fort Benton, but not often." Then she clapped her hands excitedly, like a little girl. "Oh, Tod I hope it's one of the big ones!"

I had seen pictures of the floating palaces that plied the Mississippi, but the boat that came churning around the bend was a disappointment. As it huffed along, its sternwheel slapping the water, it was not great shakes for my money. They say those boats can run on a heavy dew. Well, this one was flat enough, dingy and cluttered with bales and cases, with cords of wood piled high aft the cabins. It worked hard to claw upstream against the heavy current.

Sunny was fluttering a handkerchief at the few passengers. Then the pilot saw us. The boat veered hard over, riding the far bank as close as it could—too close, for it struck a sandbar with a loud thump. Bells jangled; the wheel, in reverse, threw great masses of spray, and the boat slid back into deeper water, and then to midstream before it could forge ahead. On its side we read the name *Bachelor* in ornate gold-leafed letters. The passengers on deck scurried for cover.

"Ahoy, there!" John Starr hailed. "Did you see any men downriver?"

A bearded face was thrust from a window of the pilothouse. The man shook a fist at us. "Ye don't trick me, ye scuts! Make a move and ye'll regret it. I've got armed men aboard here."

"Don't worry; we *are* the law," John Starr called. "We're on the trail of outlaws. Any sign of such below here?"

"Seen two men, ten mile down. Shot at us and busted a window, the rapscallions!"

"Only two? No mounted band?"

"That's all—no band—of men—anywhere …"

The pilot's voice died away as the boat churned upstream at its best speed. I can't say the steamboat men weren't smart, running fast, for there were plenty of hardcases along the big river, Indians and 'breeds and renegade whites. Not big enough to be true outlaws, but vicious nevertheless. I watched the boat until it went out of sight around the bend. For some time we could mark its plume of black smoke among the distant cottonwoods.

"Ain't likely an outlaw army would show itself, anyhow," young Paterson said. "They might duck when the boat passed."

John Starr drew a knuckle across his mustache. "I was counting on them," he said.

"How's that, Starr?" Adams asked in surprise.

"We'd have them all together. And we'd make the final accounting right here where it began. Now I don't know.

John Starr had planted the seed. I watched it grow.

"Dam' if you ain't right," Adams said angrily. "Here's these men been riding roughshod over our country the last four years—thieves, murderers, and worse. They'll be taken into court in Miles City or Helena or such, and likely they'll go free. Or spend a year or two in Deer Lodge at the most, to come out and kill and rob again."

"I've seen it," Taylor said. "A bunch of townies on the jury, don't know sic'em about the cattle range. Some old biddy says

'Oh, those pore boys, they didn't mean no wrong.' And they turn 'em loose. Then we got all the hard ridin' and the lead whizzin' around our ears again. Only, this time we try 'em in a cattle court."

"What do you think Fischel would do, Starr, if we asked him to shut his eyes?" Reece Anderson asked.

"He'll protest. But how long or how loud I don't know."

"I know Fischel," Taylor said. "He's a straight shooter and a good officer. But he knows the range. With a show of force ..."

Mrs. Lowall came forward. "John, don't do it, please. Don't be party to another lynching. Hasn't all this cruelty and death gone far enough?"

There was a cold edge to Starr's voice when he spoke. "Beth, you have to play the hand the way the cards fall. I want you to take Sunny and ride back toward Lazy L. Alone."

Her head high, she defied him. "John, the brush that tars you will tar me as well."

"So be it," he said curtly. Then he shook his head. "Those men the steamer spotted were probably Bent Lowall and Shan Kiley. Go round 'em up, Tod. And take the girl with you."

"That's too dangerous for her," I said hotly. "Besides, you'll need me here."

"Take her, Tod," Beth pleaded. "Get her away from here!"

"I'm not going—" I began.

"Tod!" John Starr's voice cracked like a whip. "Git gone. I won't tell you again."

It was a tone that my uncle seldom used. It made the hair rise on the back of my neck. Without argument, I helped Sunny up on the dun, then swung onto Blackie and rode into the brush on the downriver trail. I didn't even dare to look back.

NINETEEN

SOME WAY DOWN the river the trail widened. Sunny rode up beside me.

"Tod, will John Starr really hang those men?"

"Higher than Haman," I said grimly.

"But he'll be going against the law."

"Listen, kid," I said, "for years John Starr has been the law. He enforced it with the muzzles of those two black guns of his. He has collected a dozen times for an awful thing that happened many years ago. And it looks like the end isn't in sight yet."

"Can't he change? Tod, my mother loves him. But if he does this thing…"

My wisdom was narrow, but I had an answer. "Sunny, a woman in love will forgive anything. And as for this rough justice your mother calls a lynching, well, John Starr has right on his side. These are known, marked criminals. They will be getting only what they deserve. The whole range country, Grant Stevens included, will applaud Starr."

"I hope you're right."

"But there is one thing your mother won't forgive—and I don't think you will either. And that is, if, for his sins, we have to punish your brother."

"I know, I know," she said wildly. "Oh, Tod, will this never end? I hate it—all of it."

"I don't know how it will end," I told her, and rode ahead.

I was watchful now. If I had been alone, and Bent Lowall hadn't been a Lowall, I might have met him and Kiley head on.

But since my uncle had palmed Sunny off on me, I must use other tactics. I held Blackie to a gentle walk, listening, listening. We went six miles, seven miles; still we did not meet them. Then, suddenly Blackie's head came up. He snorted. I reined him down. Handing the reins to Sunny, I dismounted.

"Stay here," I told her. "I'm depending on you. I might come boiling back like the devil himself was after me. Be ready."

I eeled into the brush beside the trail, trying to ignore the clouds of hungry mosquitoes that swarmed in the lowlands. I cut around a little slough, found a downed cottonwood for a bridge over a creek and, with the trail still in sight, wormed over a low ridge. I looked down on a small open park.

Two horses cropped on the lush grass. In a spot of shade, barely visible in the tall grass, I made out two figures. Moving closer, I listened.

"Bent, I say it again, you're yellow. I seen it when we worked over the Injun, long time ago, you pukin' like a whey-faced girl. You didn' like it, me stringin' up Lecky an' ole Bart Stoker. You didn' like it, huh?"

"Jus' got weak stomach, Shan. You my pal, ole pal. Gimme that bot'l'. Makes me feel good. Like I'm nine feet tall."

I saw Bent Lowall teeter to his feet, tipping a bottle. He nearly strangled, then tried again. "Ole Lecky had good stuff, Shan. Glad we took it. He didn' need it; he's dead. Lecky's dead. Wish the Stranglers were too."

"They will be. Even if not one of my pa's good friends showed up where he shoulda been. Bent, we gotta resicue him ourse'fs. Shoot down the goddam swaddies; shoot down the U.S. Marshall. We ain't yellowbellies. Shoot 'em all."

"Hooray!" Bent Lowall cried. He staggered, caught his heel, and sat down hard.

I stepped into sight and stood with my thumbs hooked in my cartridge belt. "Having fun, boys?" I asked.

Though Shan Kiley was half drunk, he came out of the grass like a diamondback, drawing his six-shooter as he came. For half an instant I held square on his heart. At the last split fraction of a second I swung my gun and shot his pistol out of his hand. He stood there stupidly clutching his wrist and staring at the trickle of blood where slivers of lead had cut his hand.

Bent sat where he had fallen. As he started to raise the bottle to his lips, I smashed it with a bullet. With utter astonishment he stared at the jagged bottleneck he held. Finally he opened his fingers and let it fall.

Keeping them covered, I eased over to Kiley's horse and slipped the lass' rope from the saddle. As I moved up to Shan, he snarled at me like a rasped tomcat. Remembering Lecky and Bart Stoker, I slashed my gunsight down his cheek, twisting it. He screamed.

I rammed the muzzle into his belly, hard. "Make one move, you cheap gunslinger, and I'll kill you," I told him. "It's too much trouble taking you in."

I tied him up ruthlessly, all double knots cinched tight, then boosted him into his saddle. He sat there cowed, the crimson from his slashed cheek dripping on his shirt. His horse didn't like the smell of it.

I walked over to Lowall. "Get up." He obeyed. I took his wrist in a come-along grip and walked him toward the sandy riverbank some three feet above the water. I stood him on the edge. Then drawing back, I booted him in the rump as hard as I could kick. He sailed through the air spread out like a huge frog, and landed with a tremendous splash. He went clean under. For a minute I wondered if he could swim. But finally he came up, sputtering and blowing, making his way toward the bank. When the current began carrying him downstream, he got panicky. I held out a broken branch and pulled him to shore.

He struggled up the bank, then sprawled in the long grass, panting. The swim seemed to have sobered him, as I had planned.

"That dam' water's cold," he chattered.

"Riding will warm you up," I told him, thrusting him toward his horse.

We were ready to go when Sunny came into the clearing. Bent's eyes widened. "What the hell you doin' here?" he demanded.

I fetched him a clout across the mouth. "Talk like a gentleman when there's a lady present," I told him. "Your sister is with me."

We rode out with Kiley in the lead, then the girl, then Lowall and me. I kept a wary eye on the trail, though it was now almost certain that the rescue party would never materialize.

"You're in pretty deep, Lowall," I said. "The hanging of those two old men was downright murder."

"That wasn't my doing," he whined. "Sure, I was with Shan. We were riding to Burnt Rock. Shan wanted booze. Lecky wouldn't give him none. Shan cut down on the two old geezers. I didn't like the look of it, so I went out to take care of our horses. Later, when I come out of the barn, the two bodies were hanging on the gate. Made me sick, it did."

"What explanation did Kiley give?"

"Said what he said right along, that they give the information to the Stranglers that got his pa in Dutch. Said he knocked Stoker out with his gun, strung Lecky up, then come back for Stoker. Said it served 'em right, that they knew the risks for what they done."

"And you were down at the barn all the time?"

"Sure. And you ought to've seen those Crows streak out of there. They had the lodges down and were packed and gone into the north in ten minutes, I bet. Men, squaws, and papooses."

I knew he hadn't had had a hand in the killing of Stoker and Sam. I had overheard Shan admit to that.

"Yet it wasn't wrong to kill two innocent old men?"

"Innocent, hell! They squealed on men better'n themselves. Got what they had coming, I'd say."

"You know Kiley's father killed your father—or had it done."

"That's crazy, and I won't believe it! Why, we're blood brothers, Shan and me. He let me do it in a regular Injun ceremony. I tell you, you ain't going to split up Shan and me."

He was not only weak, but weak-minded. "You're so sure of that? Shan Kiley's going to hang."

His face turned greenish white. "They—they can't do that. What about me?"

"Nothing, if you keep that big mouth of yours shut from now on. Your mother is ace high with everyone, and Starr will try to keep your name out of it. But it's touch and go, Bent. You got a long rope and a tight knot coming to you. You want to duck it, you better belly down and keep quiet. Real quiet."

His hand went to his throat in an unconscious gesture. Then he wiped his mouth with the back of his hand. "I—I don't believe it," he said, his voice barely a whisper.

"You damned well better believe it, mister," I said grimly. "The ice you're on is so thin it cracks every time you draw breath. The best thing you can do is start praying. And I wouldn't let up until you're safe at Lazy L."

I dropped back. Whether he prayed or not I don't know. But his lips were moving.

We rode into the Burnt Rock clearing in midafternoon. I hauled Blackie back sharply. when I saw dismounted men. Signaling to the Lowalls to stay back, I rode forward. I saw a man I recognized.

"Hi, Bill," I said. "You just in from Poplar?"

"That we are," he said with some sarcasm. "For all the good the ride did. Ain't that young Kiley you got there? We could use him. Bring back one prisoner, anyhow."

"I'm holding him for John Starr," I said.

"You could turn him over to Fischel, here," he told me. "He's a depitty U.S. Marshal. Matter of fact, all of us is, special fer the occasion. With warrants, too. Much good it did."

"Your man Starr packs mighty potent warrants himself," Fischel said wearily. "One on each hip. Though the Army won't like it."

"I suppose not. But what about your men?"

"Unofficially, the higher John Starr hangs them, the better. Sick as they were, and leakin' with bullet holes, they made us near throw up with their brag all the way from Poplar. Some of the things they told about..." He paused, shaking his head. "And I s'pose they were true, too. Rotten renegades. That's unofficial, remember."

"I know. And you might forget the name of John Starr."

"We'll try, though I don't think he gives a damn," Fischel said, grinning. "We made it across the ford, and there he was, aiming those two cannons square down our throats. I'd heard of Starr. He's not a man to argue with. We didn't. The prisoners weren't happy, I tell you."

"Who were they?"

"Rance Kiley, Paddy Rose, Burr, and Nickerson. A fine hand to draw to—all cards wild."

"No doubt Starr is on his way to Fort Maginnis with them," I said straightfaced.

"No doubt; and I'm sure you'll want to deliver this one to the major at the same time," Fischel said ironically.

"I would if I knew their trail," I told him.

Bill swung an arm. "South and west, when they started. Say, that Starr—he don't like the human race much, does he?"

Once again I found myself defending my uncle. "He's bucked so many criminals his mind runs on a single track: you can make a bad man good only by killing him."

"After a day and night with four of 'em, I'm inclined to agree," Fischel said. "There's much can be said for his point of view. And

I'll add one thing—he sure as hell has the courage of his convictions." The Marshal and I walked over to my group.

"Marshal, I want you to take me into custody; I'll ride with you to the fort and surrender," Shan said.

"Afraid not, mister," Fischel told him. "You're in good hands now."

"But they aim to hang me!" Kiley cried.

"You'll have company," Fischel assured him. He shook hands with me, gave Sunny an admiring look, and walked away.

"Let's go," I said.

On the trail Kiley asked, "Was my pa took, too?"

"He was," I told him. "Wounded, they said, but not too bad."

He rode on ahead then, his hands twisting under the rawhide bonds. But I had tied them myself, and I knew it was of no use for Kiley to struggle with them.

When the trail widened, Sunny and Bent Lowall rode up beside me. "Tod, if Shan promised to head for the border and never come back, would you turn him loose?" Sunny asked.

I shook my head. "It might have been possible until he murdered Lecky and old Bart. But your own brother is a witness to that. Besides, more than one innocent man has been killed by this gang. Kiley must hang."

"What good will another dead man do the country?" she flared. "I—I don't want blood on your hands."

"It's part of cleaning up the country so it's fit to live in," I said gently. "Sunny, men can't live under a reign of terror. I'll admit that John Starr's way is harsh. But it is quick, effective, and—permanent."

Some of the bluster was coming back in Lowall. "Well, I don't like Starr," he said. "I've watched him hanging around my mother. I'll put a spoke in his wheel, you wait and see."

"Don't tangle with Starr," I warned him. "You're on the ragged edge now. Don't cross him. These are desperate times. A man like you who gets in the way might get hurt."

"I ain't afraid of John Starr. I'll stick with my blood brother Shan. Starr don't scare me."

"Then you're a fool," I said bluntly. "Sunny, talk some sense into him."

Sunny said: "Bent, did you ever stop to think how strange it might look to an outsider for you to claim that one man hanged two grown men, all by himself?"

Lowall jerked around. "But that's what happened! You lay off me. I was down at the barn all the time, I told you!"

"You know how tough and how strong your pal Shan is. But your story might seem odd, let us say, to John Starr. Perhaps you'd better keep quiet entirely, and let Tod do the talking."

He stared at her. "Maybe you're right. I won't say anything."

"My blood brother!" Shan jeered.

TWENTY

A s WE RODE over a rolling ridge, we saw Finn Spring, a rock sink with an old wolfer's cabin and sheds nearby. Riders clustered around the building. We came down the slope at a trot.

John Starr moved out of the group and waved an arm.

I yelled at Sunny, "Stay back! You too, Bent."

Prodding Shan Kiley before me, I rode up to my uncle.

"Is it over?" I asked.

He nodded. "All four of 'em. Behind the cabin."

"You devil!" Shan cried. "You killed my pa!"

"Executed him, rather," Starr said calmly. "Beckett! Come here and guard this man."

Red Beckett took the bridle reins of both horses. I swung down and walked with Starr around the building. Though I was prepared, my stomach gave a lurch when I saw the four bodies dangling from a long timber braced between barn and cabin. Strangely elongated, they swung and twisted slowly in the light breeze. I turned away.

Starr's face was drawn. "They earned it, Tod," he said. "But, for the first time, I felt no satisfaction at the end of the trail. Too many such men—too much blood..." He was silent, looking through and beyond me with sad eyes.

"What about young Kiley?" I asked. "He's guilty as hell. He killed both Lecky and Stoker, according to Bent Lowall and his own admission. I heard him."

"Bent had no hand in it?"

"He says."

"We'll whitewash him, then. I'd do anything on God's green earth for that boy's mother. This is the last. I'm hanging up my guns. If Beth Lowall will have me, I'll marry her."

"That'll be the smartest thing you've ever done in your life, Uncle John," I said. "But what now?"

He looked grim. "You take Bent and the girl just over the hill. Beth is waiting there, worrying about her cub, no doubt. With his bad companions gone, Bent may straighten up."

"That's a lot to hope for," I grumbled. "You'll join us there?"

"As soon as I can.

We walked toward the horses.

"All right, Tod. Ride," John Starr said. "Red, bring on Kiley. His own horse will do."

"What are you going to do?" Bent cried.

"Hang him for his sins," John Starr said. "You know that, Bent."

"You can't! He's my blood brother!"

"You stop 'em, Bent," Kiley said sarcastically. I had to admire his acceptance of the inevitable.

"Let's ride," I said. "So long, Kiley."

"To hell with you," Kiley snarled. "And you too—blood brother!"

I gave Lowall's horse a slap on the rump. As we galloped away, I heard Kiley say, "Come on, you sons of bitches; let's get it over with."

We found Beth Lowall near a little spring in a glade down the trail from the cabin. She was sitting on the grass, the skirt of her riding habit spread around her. As we rode up, she leaped to her feet, joy written on her face at the sight of her son.

He sprang down and ran to her. Grown man though he was, she folded him in her arms. They stood there, rocking a little, his face buried in her shoulder. Across him, she looked at me with a question. I nodded, spreading my hands in a gesture of finality. I saw the tears spring to her eyes.

Lowall broke away. "That Starr is a murderer, Mother!" he cried. "He hung Nickerson and Burr and Rance Kiley and Paddy Rose. And he's hanging my friend Shan. Right now!"

"John Starr is a good man," she rebuked him. "Your so-called friends were thieves and murderers, Bent. and you know it. It's only because of Starr and Tod Morgan that you didn't find death in a noose this afternoon."

"But I didn't do anything! Yet they threatened to hang me."

There was anger in Beth Lowall's voice. "You're a man now, Benton. You can't hide behind my skirts forever. This was a harsh lesson, but you'd better learn from it—and learn well. This time was the last."

"So they've even turned you against me! But just the same, Shan Kiley is—was—a better man than any of them!"

"Shan Kiley was a murdering thief—" I began angrily. But Beth silenced me with a gesture.

"Enough, Tod," she said. "I think Benton, in spite of his bluster, knows how lucky he is. Isn't that John riding this way?"

"It is," I answered. I moved closer to her, and said softly, "He's hanging up his guns."

She put a hand on my arm. "Tod, don't ever get the wrong view of your uncle. He was killed, yes. But he has made many areas of the West safe for decent people. I know John Starr is a fine man. His guns go silent, not because of my wish, but because of something within himself, something fine in the very soul of him. Tod, I love that man."

Awed at the depth of her feeling, I started to answer; but, her face aglow, she was already walking through the tall, flower-starred grass toward my uncle.

Sunny said, "Tod, I hope that means you will stay, too. In this country, I mean."

"Could be," I said, watching the two across the glade. "I might just consider it."

She smiled, and with a shy, tentative motion, touched her soft fingers to my cheek.

As my uncle and Beth came toward us through the glade, their faces shining with happiness, I heard Benton Lowall say, "Starr!"

I turned in surprise to see him walking slowly toward my uncle, his face haggard, his eyes wild. Suddenly, mouthing a wordless cry, Lowall snatched his hand from his pocket. Then with a little hideout gun, he shot John Starr twice in the chest.

"I'll show you!" he yelled.

Too late, I realized that he was mad.

Too late, I made the fastest draw I will ever make in my life. I killed Benton Lowall in his tracks.

For a hideous moment the whole world stopped. Then Beth ran forward. For a second she stood between the two bodies. Then she made her decision. She dropped to her knees beside Benton Lowall.

"Oh, my son, my son!" she cried, stark agony in her voice.

I went to Starr. He was moaning a little, blood flecking his lips. As I raised his head, his eyes opened.

"You know me now, Tod," he whispered. "This is the way—vengeance trail—comes to its end. Beth—my love ... Tod—don't follow it—don't—" His head dropped back, and he was gone.

I stood up, my soul sick as I looked beyond my uncle's body, at the carrion that had done this thing.

From beside her brother's body Sunny stood up. The sinking sun caught the blaze of her golden hair. She looked at me, a look of such utter contempt and loathing that the anger suddenly went out of me. The world was empty, and so was I. There was nothing there for me. I had killed it all with one quick shot from my six-gun.

I don't know if she watched or not. But I caught up my horse and rode away without a word, rode east with my long shadow reaching out across the sage ahead of me.

The chokecherry and the alder are red; the aspens are turing coin gold. In the early morning the long grass is sifted with a rime of frost. The fool hens are drifting down into the barnyard, looking for spilled grain. Here in the Shonkin the Little Rockies are just a haze far to the northeast. The Little Belts and the Highwoods are the mountains that loom large on the horizon now. Fall is on the wide land, with the long hard winter an imminent threat.

I've been breaking broncs. That's the only trade I know. I sold my guns for bar money in Lewistown. Nor do I want them back again, ever. God knows I'm not a child any more. The Kansas plowboy has gone for good now. Whatever innocence I still had left, I lost that terrible July afternoon.

Oh, I can think about it now. I still regret it. But no longer do I torture myself because I had neglected to search Bent Lowall for a hideout gun. I know now that what happened would have happened, no matter what I said or did. Maybe not in that way, but in one way or another. Nor does my conscience prick me for killing young Lowall. He was born to cause his family nothing but pain and hurt and disgrace all of his days. There are men like that.

I said I can stand off and look at the thing now. That isn't quite right. There's one bitter wound that won't quite heal.

I still remember the bright gleam of yellow hair, the music of a laugh.

Maybe Sunny was right. But I had my reasons. I had my own code and the deadly quickness of my hand. I still think I could not have done otherwise.

That's why I ride the broncs until I'm so numb I can't think. A man needs money to eat, and eat he must, even if his soul is starved. I hope the boss keeps me on J-Bar this winter—we have to feed our bellies, at least, if not our souls. Just now I saw the bull cook drive in from Fort Benton with the wagon piled high with provisions.

Here he comes now, waving some kind of paper at me.

What's all the commotion, Cookee?

A letter for me? From a Miss Sunny Lowall, you say?

Give it to me! Quick, damn you!

www.ingramcontent.com/pod-product-compliance
Lightning Source LLC
Chambersburg PA
CBHW052008240626
47153CB00008B/2783